Bengal Nights

Bengal Nights

Mircea Eliade

The University of Chicago Press

Mircea Eliade (1907–1986) was the Sewell L. Avery Distinguished
Service Professor in the Divinity School and in the Committee on
Social Thought at the University of Chicago. He was the author of
some fifty books, including novels, short stories, and plays as well as
works in the history of religions. Among his books published by the
University of Chicago Press are the four volume *Journal*, the two-
volume *Autobiography*, and the novella *The Old Man and the
Bureaucrats*.

Originally published in French as *La nuit bengali*, Editions Gallimard, 1950

The University of Chicago Press, Chicago 60637
Carcanet Press Limited, Manchester, England

Translation copyright © Catherine Spencer 1993
All rights reserved. University of Chicago Press edition 1994
Printed in Great Britain

03 02 01 00 99 98 97 96 95 94   54321
ISBN 0–226–20418–9 (cloth)

CIP data are available from the Current in Publication Division
of the Library of Congress, Washington, D.C.

This book is printed on acid-free paper

I

If I hesitate in beginning, it is because I still have not managed to remember the exact date of my first meeting with Maitreyi. I have not found anything in my notes of that year. Her name does not appear until very much later – until after I had left the sanatorium and was living with Narendra Sen in Bhowanipore. But that was in 1929 and I had already seen Maitreyi, at least ten months earlier. As I begin, I feel somewhat pained that I cannot evoke an image of her at that time or re-live the surprise, uncertainty or confusion that I experienced at our first meetings.

I have a very vague memory: Maitreyi waiting in a motor-car opposite the Oxford Book Stationery store. Her father and I were each choosing some books for Christmas. On catching sight of her, a strange tremor went through me, accompanied by a curious feeling of contempt. I thought her ugly, with eyes that were too large and too black, thick and curling lips and the powerful chest of a Bengali maiden who had developed too quickly.

We were introduced. She put the joined palms of her hands to her forehead in greeting and all at once I saw her bare arm. The colour of her skin struck me – it was a shade I had never seen before: matt brown, an alloy of clay and wax.

I was living at that time at Ripon Mansions, in Wellesley Street. One Harold Carr, an employee of the Army and Navy Stores, had the room next to mine. We were good friends. He knew many families in Calcutta, and we spent our evenings with these people. Once a week we took girls dancing.

I wanted to describe to Harold – to see it more clearly for

myself rather than to inform him – Maitreyi's naked arm and
the strange quality of that sombre brown, so disturbing and so
unfeminine; it was the flesh of a goddess or a painted image
rather than of a human. Harold was shaving in front of a mirror,
his foot propped up on a low table. I can picture the scene now:
the tea-cups, his wax-stained purple pyjamas (he had beaten
his servant bloody for that, but it was he who had made the
mess himself, returning home drunk one night from the
YMCA ball), some nickel coins on the unmade bed – and
me, trying in vain to unblock my pipe with a piece of paper
that I had rolled as thinly as a matchstick.

"Really, Alain, how could you fall for a Bengali? They're
disgusting. I was born here, I know these women better than
you do. They are dirty – and there's nothing doing, believe me,
no question of love! That girl will never look at you."

Because I had obligingly described a girl's arm to him, he was
already imagining that my mind was on love. Like all the Anglo-
Indians, Harold was an idiot and a fanatic, but his inane diatribe
against Bengali women made a curious impression on me. I had
the vague feeling that the memory of Maitreyi was already
connected in some way to my most fugitive thoughts and
desires... The idea both amused and disturbed me. I walked
back to my room, still trying, mechanically, to unblock my pipe.

I noted nothing in my diary at the time. It was only very
much later – the night I received the little sprig of jasmine –
that I revived those first impressions.

I was just beginning my career in India. I had arrived full of
superstitions: a member of the Rotary Club, very proud of my
nationality and my continental origins. I devoured books on
mathematical physics (although as a child I had wanted to
become a missionary) and devoted much attention to my private journal. At first, I worked as a sales representative for the
Noel and Noel factories, but soon afterwards I joined the new
delta canalization project as a draughtsman. That was how I
met Narendra Sen, Maitreyi's father, a man who enjoyed great

renown in Calcutta – he was the first Bengali engineer to have
won an award from Edinburgh University. My life changed. I
earned less but the work pleased me. I no longer had to simmer
away dutifully in the Clive Street offices, to sign or wade
through an infinity of documents or get drunk every night to
obliterate my depression.

I was responsible for the works at Tamluk and I went away
every two or three weeks. Each time I arrived at the site, my
heart would fill with satisfaction at the sight of the dykes
growing ever higher.

Those months were truly happy. I would take the Howrah–
Madras express at dawn and arrive before breakfast. I have
always loved journeys in the colonies, and to travel first class
in India is a veritable excursion into pleasure. The station
became a friend. Every departure was the same. I would jump
out of the taxi and dash, wide awake, on to the platform, my
brown cap pulled down over my eyes, my servant behind me,
five illustrated magazines under my arm and two packets of
Capstan in my hand. I smoked a lot at Tamluk and I was always
worried that I had not brought enough cigarettes with me. The
memory of a night when I had nothing for my pipe other than
the workers' foul mixture made me shudder. I never spoke to
my fellow travellers. I was not fond of the *burra*-sahibs,
mediocre Oxford graduates, rich young Indians, devotees of
the detective story, who had learnt to travel first class but who
did not know how to wear a jacket or use a toothpick. From the
window I admired those Bengal plains which have never
inspired a song in anyone, much less a complaint, and in this
way, silent and without desire, I nursed my solitude.

As the only white man, I was sole master on the site. The
Anglo-Indians, who were supervising the work near the bridge,
did not enjoy the same prestige as I. They travelled third class,
wore the traditional khaki suits – short trousers and jackets with
large pockets – and could insult the workers in a perfect
Hindustani. Their mastery of the language and their rich

vocabulary lowered them in the eyes of their subordinates. I, on the contrary, spoke badly, with a deplorable accent – my superiority was therefore indisputable. But I also spoke freely with these people in the evenings, before retiring into my tent to write, to smoke a last pipe, to meditate.

I loved that piece of ground near the sea, that snake-infested, deserted plain where palm-trees intertwined with heavily perfumed undergrowth. I loved those tranquil sunrises, the stillness that tore cries of joy out of me. A joyous solitude reigned over this green and abundant land, which waited silently for its passing travellers to arrive under the most beautiful skies that it had ever been my lot to witness.

Days spent at the site seemed like holidays. I had a taste for the work, giving orders left and right, filled with good humour. If I had had a single intelligent companion with me, I would have had marvellous things to tell him.

I met Lucien Metz by chance. It was on one of those trips back from Tamluk, from which I would return sunburnt and devoured by a lunatic hunger. I was waiting at the entrance of the station while my servant called a taxi for me; the Bombay express had just got in and there was an unimaginable crowd.

I had met Lucien two years earlier. My ship, *en route* for India, had made a port of call at Aden for a few hours, where he was waiting for an Italian steamer to return to Egypt. I had liked the uncultured, arrogant journalist, with his talent and his perspicacity, from the very first. He had written an article about political economy when he was on board ship, simply by going through a list of prices and comparing them to those of the ports; after an hour's drive around a town, he could describe it in perfect detail. He had visited India, China, Malaysia and Japan several times. He was one of the rare Europeans who reproached Gandhi not for what he was doing but for what he was failing to do.

"Hey, Alain," he shouted, not seeming in the least surprised to see me. "So, still in India, my friend? Tell this fellow, who is pretending he doesn't understand my English, to take me to the YMCA and not a hotel. I've come to write a book on India. Cross between politics and thriller. It's going to be a bestseller. I'll have to tell you about it."

And so it was. Lucien wanted to write a book on modern India. For several months he had collected interviews, visited prisons, taken photographs. That evening, he began showing me his album and his notes. What troubled him was his chapter on women. He had not yet encountered "real Indian women"; he vaguely knew something of their life in purdah, had a few notions about their civic rights and was especially interested in child marriage. He asked me several times:

"Alain, is it true these people marry little girls of eight? Yes, yes! I read it in a book by a man who spent thirty years here as a magistrate..."

We spent an enjoyable evening on the hostel terrace. Despite all my efforts, I could not teach him much. I knew barely more than he about the women of India. Except at functions or the cinema, I hardly saw them.

An idea struck me. My excellent relationship with Mr Sen was confined to our work together in the office and conversations in his car; he had twice invited me to tea, but I had been too attached to my leisure hours, entirely consecrated to mathematical physics, and had declined. Now I would suggest to him that he invite the journalist to tea, so that he could give him some first-hand information. Perhaps I also wanted the opportunity of observing Maitreyi more closely... I had not seen her since our brief encounter outside the store.

I told him that Lucien Metz was writing a book on India that would be published in Paris and I intimated the problems my friend was having with one of the chapters. He at once invited us to come for tea, that very afternoon. With what excitement I climbed the hostel stairs to tell Lucien the good news! He had never been to the house of a rich Indian. Now his research would be complete.

"Your Sen, what caste does he belong to?" he asked.

"He's a genuine Brahmin, but as unorthodox as they come.
He's a founding member of the Rotary Club, plays a marvellous
game of tennis, drives his own car, eats fish and meat, invites
Europeans to his house and introduces them to his wife. I know
you'll like him."

I have to admit that I was as surprised as Lucien. I knew the
outside of the engineer's house in Bhowanipore: I had driven to
the district to collect some plans. Yet I would never have imagined that the interior of a Bengal house could contain so many
marvels, so much light filtered through curtains as translucent as
chiffon shawls, so many rugs soft to the touch, so many sofas
draped in cashmere and curious little one-legged tables bearing
plates of beaten copper. Placed on these tables were tea cups and
cakes that Narendra Sen himself had chosen to best introduce
his guest to Indian pastry. Rooted to the spot, I stood gazing at
the living-room as though I had that very moment disembarked
in India. I had spent two years in this country and I had never
been curious to enter the house of a Bengali family, to penetrate
their private lives and admire their works of art, if not their souls.
I had led the life of a solitary colonial, taken up with my work at
the site or the office, reading or going to shows that I could just as
well have seen in white continents. That afternoon, I experienced my first doubts about my way of life. I remember that I
went home rather despondent.

Lucien, full of enthusiasm, interrogated me on this or that
detail, wanting to know if he had correctly understood his host.
I myself had been invaded by an army of new ideas. I noted
nothing down, however, and I cannot find any reference to the
impression Maitreyi made on me that day. I can no longer
remember my feelings with any accuracy. It is remarkable that
I did not foresee, that afternoon, the events which were to come
or recognize the characters who were to change the whole
shape of my life.

Maitreyi had appeared much more beautiful to me then than

at our first meeting – in her sari the colour of weak tea, her white slippers woven with silver thread and her burnished yellow shawl. The hair that was too black, the eyes that were too large, the lips that were too red, inhabited this veiled body with a life that was somehow inhuman, miraculous and hardly real. I contemplated her quizzically. I could not fathom the mystery that lay hidden in this creature of movements as supple as silk, whose timid smile was never far from panic, whose musical voice continually invented new harmonies, new pitches. Maitreyi's English was quaint and formal, somewhat scholarly, yet she had only to open her mouth and Lucien and I felt ourselves forced to look at her. Her words pulled us like the calls of a siren.

The tea was rich in surprises. Lucien took notes after tasting each one of the sweetmeats and did not stop asking questions. His English was bad. Sen, however, had assured him that he understood French – he had attended two conferences in Paris and had a library full of French novels, although he had not read any of them – and Lucien questioned him from time to time in Parisian slang. The engineer smilingly replied "Oui, oui, c'est ça," with an air of great self-satisfaction.

Lucien asked permission to examine Maitreyi's costume, her jewels and ornaments, more closely and Narendra Sen accepted with good grace, leading his daughter over by the hand: frightened, she had drawn back near the window, her lips quivering, her shawl pulled over her head. It was a strange examination. Lucien weighed up the jewels in his hand, giving exclamations of wonder, asked questions and took down the answers in shorthand. During all this, Maitreyi stood, her face ashen, trembling from head to foot as though stricken with pure terror. She did not know where to look. Then her eyes met mine. I smiled at her. She seemed to have found a haven; fixing her gaze on mine, she gradually became calmer, her spasms ceased and she began to recover her normal state. I do not know how long that look lasted. It was not like any other that

I had ever experienced. The examination over, Maitreyi once more took refuge by the window. We did not look at each other again, after that warm and clandestine moment of communion.

I turned my attention to her father and from my vantage point I analysed him at leisure. I wondered how a man could be so ugly, could lack expression so completely. He resembled a frog: bulging eyes, enormous mouth, round, black, iron pot of a head, low forehead and jet-black curls, squat body and sloping shoulders, protruding belly, short legs. The affection that this man inspired was difficult to comprehend – and yet I, too, found Narendra Sen a seductive being, sensitive and intelligent, full of humour, gentleness and loyalty.

Whilst I had been studying him in this way, his wife Srimati Devi Indira had entered the room, bringing with her some strange atmosphere of warmth and fear. She was wearing a blue sari and a blue shawl sequined with gold. Her feet were bare; the soles and the toes were decorated with henna. She knew almost no English and smiled continually in place of speech. She had doubtlessly chewed a lot of pan that afternoon, for her lips were blood red. She astounded me. She seemed so young, so fresh and timid, that I would have taken her for Maitreyi's elder sister rather than her mother. Chabu, her second daughter, had come in with her. She was a child of about eleven, short-haired and dressed in the European style, but without socks or shoes. Her bare calves and arms and her swarthy, sweet face reminded me of one of our European gypsies.

I find it almost impossible to recount the incident that then took place. The three women had huddled up together on the couch, each with the same expression of terror in her eyes, while the engineer tried in vain to make them speak. The mistress of the house wanted to pour the tea, but she changed her mind and entrusted the task to her elder daughter.

Suddenly, the teapot was knocked over on to the tray – I do not know whose fault it was – and Lucien's trousers were drenched. Everyone rushed to his aid while the engineer, his equanimity quite gone, berated his family sharply in Bengali. Lucien, for his part, stood apologising in French without managing to make himself understood. Narendra Sen finally gestured for him to sit down again, saying, "'Scusez moi! Ici votre place." The girls ran at once to change the silk chair-cover and their father continued to scold them. Lucien and I sat dumbly, not knowing what to do with our hands nor where to look. My friend was quite flushed with embarrassment – although on the way back to the hostel he laughed the incident off loudly. Only Mrs Sen remained impassive, the same smile on her reddened lips, the same warm shyness in her eyes.

The conversation hardly revived. The engineer showed Lucien some ancient Sanskrit texts that had belonged in the collection of his uncle, who had been the first government 'pandit', and then a series of pictures and old embroideries. I had gone to stand by the window and I looked out at the courtyard, a curious place closed in by high walls and planted with small shrubs and wisteria. From the side of the house, above me, drifted the fragile scent of a palm-tree. I contemplated the view, uncertain of the origin of this enchantment, this tranquillity which I had never before experienced in Calcutta. And suddenly I heard an irresistible, contagious laugh, the laugh of both a woman and a child. It gripped my heart, and I shivered. I leaned out of the window and beheld, stretched out across two steps of the courtyard stairs, Maitreyi, almost naked, her hair in her eyes, her arms clasped over her chest. I saw her move her legs, quite shaken with laughter, and then, with a brisk jerk of her ankles, throw off her two slippers against the wall opposite. I stood transfixed, unable to avert my eyes. Those few moments seemed eternal. I felt that laugh and the wild flame of that unleashed body to be somehow sacred and I was certain that I was committing a sacrilege by witnessing them. Yet I did not have the strength to tear myself away.

As we were leaving, Maitreyi's laugh echoed through the house.

II

I was at Tamluk, where I had gone upstream to walk.

Two days earlier, Norinne had got engaged and we had celebrated all night. We had drunk too much, danced until we were dizzy, kissed all the girls and driven off in the small hours to the lakes. We had also planned a pyjama party, like the one we had held the previous March, when I quarrelled with Eddie Higgering and came to blows. I had loved Norinne for a while, as we loved then, youngsters of twenty-four; I would willingly have held her in my arms, I would have danced with her – a few kisses and that was all.

I walked along tranquilly, my pipe in one hand and my stick in the other. The sun had not yet set the place alight, birds were chirping in the large bushes of eglantine and the air was heavy with their perfume of incense and cinnamon. Suddenly, in a flash of illumination, I grasped my extraordinary condition. I was alone and I would die alone. The thought did not sadden me. Rather, I felt quiet, serene, at peace with the surrounding plain. If someone had told me I was to die in an hour, I would have accepted my fate calmly. I would have lain back in the grass, put my hands behind my head and, my eyes fixed on the blue ocean above me, waited for the time to run out, without counting the minutes or wanting to hurry them, almost without being conscious of them.

I do not know what instinctive and superhuman sense of majesty filled me. I could have done anything -- although all desire had left me. It was as though my appetite for solitude in this enchanted ground had made me light-headed. I thought of

Norinne, of Harold, of all the others, and I wondered how they could have entered my life, what meaning their existence – so dull and so mediocre – could have beside mine. I walked, lost in thought.

I went back to the site still hungry for seclusion and peace. I looked forward to the prospect of staying in my tent for a week – a week in which I would not read any magazines or see a single electric light bulb. The servant came to meet me.

"Sahib, there is a telegram from Calcutta."

I thought it must concern some materials to be collected and I was in no hurry to read it. However, when eventually I had opened it, I stood surprised and disconcerted for several minutes. Narendra Sen was calling me back urgently to headquarters. I was to take the train that evening.

It was with a feeling of heavy sadness that I sat at the window of my carriage and contemplated the steam-covered plain, filled with the diaphanous shadows of lone palm trees – the landscape which had welcomed me that morning, with such generosity, into the heart of its existence outside limits of time, beyond aims and conclusions. How I wished I were free, sitting in my tent by the light of a petrol lamp and listening to the huge orchestra of cicadas and grasshoppers around me.

"Alain, I have good news for you," Narendra Sen said to me when we arrived back at the office. "We need a capable man to inspect the earthworks and the bridges on the Lumding-Sadyia line. I thought of you at once, and the board has accepted you, under its own responsibility. You have three days to sort out your affairs and to hand over to your successor at Tamluk."

He looked at me with an expression of extreme kindness and his ugly face lit up with a warm affection that I found acutely embarrassing. I was to discover later that he had waged a hard battle with the board to have me, a white man, taken on. The company was swarajist and wanted to filter out the last of its foreign employees, to replace them with Indians. My new post was both higher in rank and better paid. Instead of 250 rupees a

month, I would earn 400, exceeding even the salary of a sales
representative for Noel and Noel. I was reluctant to work in
Assam, a region that was unhealthy and barely civilized.
However, my love for the jungle, which I had brought with
me to India and which I had not yet been able to satisfy,
triumphed. I accepted the offer and thanked him warmly.

The engineer put his hand on my shoulder:

"My wife and I like you very much, Alain, and we often think
of you. It is a pity you do not speak Bengali..."

At the time, I did not reflect on any of this very deeply. I did
indeed wonder – but only vaguely – why the engineer had
chosen me, over all his compatriots, for the new post. The
answer I gave myself was simple: he appreciated my quali-
ties. I had a clear opinion of my talent for construction, my
position as white civilizer and the service which I was rendering
to India.

When Harold learnt the news of my promotion in rank and
salary, he at once wanted to celebrate with a small banquet in
China Town. We invited some girls to come with us and set off
in two taxis. Our group was noisy, bubbling over with high
spirits and frivolity. Coming out of Park Street on to
Chowringhee Road, our two cars raced each other, each team
shouting at the driver and tapping him on the shoulder to spur
him on. Our charioteer was a magnificent Sikh who had fought
in France during the war and he cried "Diable! Diable! Vin
rouge! Vin blanc!" in his excitement. Gertie was sitting on my
knees, clutching me with terror (she knew that I had just had a
tidy increase in salary), repeating over and over: "I'm going to
fall. Aren't you afraid I'll fall?"

At the junction of Dhurmtollah Street, we had to stop to wait
for a tram to pass. The others were gaining on us and we were
dismayed at this unfortunate turn of events. At that moment, a
car passed us and with horror I saw inside Narendra Sen, his
wife and Maitreyi. I blushed like a fool as I greeted them, and
Sen smiled back at me with something of contempt. Mrs Sen

shot me a glance of terror and stupefaction that I could not interpret. Maitreyi alone brought her palms to her forehead and returned my salutation. She appeared infinitely amused by the merry company around me and by the girl in my arms. I wanted to execute an Indian greeting in return but all at once I realized the ludicrousness of my situation. My panic lasted until our car moved off again. I turned, and caught sight of Maitreyi's shawl floating in the wind, the colour of weak tea.

My friends enjoyed themselves hugely over the respect and the embarrassment with which I had greeted a 'black'. "You'll be running to bathe in the Ganges next!" Gertie threw out maliciously.

Poor Harold, shocked at me once more, asked how I could be so friendly with a family of 'negroes'. The driver, however, was visibly exultant. When I paid him in front of the restaurant, he said to me in French, so the others would not understand, "Girl very nice, Sahib. Bahut accha!"

When I arrived at the office the next morning, Narendra Sen asked me in the most natural of tones:

"Who were you with last night, Alain?"

"Some friends, sir," I replied, excessively polite.

"But the girl on your lap? She was very beautiful. Do you love her?"

"Those girls come too cheaply to love, Mr Sen. I had to take my friends out for a farewell party and as there were many of us, we economized by not taking a third taxi. Everyone had a girl on his lap. There was nothing untoward, sir, or at least..."

I tailed off. It was obvious that, he found this litany of explanations excessive. He slapped me on the shoulder.

"You have other paths open to you, Alain. You are worth more than this Anglo-Indian way of life. This hostel life will ruin you – you will never learn to love India if you live with these people."

I was astonished at the interest the engineer was suddenly showing in my private life. Until then, he had asked only if I were getting used to the food, if I had a good servant, if I were not suffering too much from the heat or the noise, if I liked tennis. We got down to work quickly. I had a pile of documents to sign. When it was time to leave, Sen asked me to dine with him at the Rotary Club. None of my objections – that I was not properly dressed, that I was tired – satisfied him and I was forced to accept. By the end of the evening, however, I was not sorry I had come. The admiration that the engineer's speech won from the distinguished audience was new proof that the man who had invited me to his table was of great worth and I felt that some of his glory must reflect on to me.

I left for Shillong that same night. Only Harold accompanied me to the station, giving me some final advice: to beware of snakes, leprosy, malaria and stomach troubles.

"Drink brandy soda and whisky soda!" he cried, as he stood waving me goodbye.

III

Today I leafed through my diary at length and re-read the pages written during my time in Assam. What great pains I had taken in deciphering my daily notes, to transfer them to the journal which began with my new life! I was filled with the strange sentiment that I was leading the life of a veritable pioneer, and my work on the construction of railway lines through the jungle seemed to me far more useful to India than a dozen books written about her. I was also sure that the encounter of this ancient world with our modern work had yet to find its novelist. I had discovered an India quite different from the one I had read about in sensational newspaper articles or books. I was living among tribes, with men who, until then, had been known only to ethnologists, amid that poisonous vegetation, under a never-ending rain and a humid and stifling heat. I wanted to give life to a region overrun by bracken and creepers, populated by men who were at once cruel and innocent. I wanted to unearth the aesthetic and ethical life of these peoples and each day I collected anecdotes, took photographs, drew up genealogies. The deeper I ventured into this wild domain, the more consuming became a hitherto unconscious notion of my superiority, the more violently assertive a pride of which I would never have believed myself capable. I was well and truly in the jungle, no longer a social being with perfect self-control.

But the rains! How many nights, tormented by depression, did I listen to the rhythmic and unforgettable sound of water falling off the roof... And those extraordinary downpours which lasted for days at a time, broken only by a few hours of very soft rain that fell like a hot spray... I would make my way through that hot-house of minute, invisible drops; unable to keep my head down, I rested it against my shoulder and ran, wrinkling my nostrils and lips against the perfumed water.

In the evenings, I would settle myself in the cool comfort of my room, or pace up and down the veranda of my bungalow, trying to rediscover the taste of my tobacco; the most minute precautions had not succeeded in protecting it from the humidity. At times I felt I could bear the life no longer. I would clench my fists, hit the balustrade with savage blows and make off under the rain into the darkness, no matter where, towards a place where the skies did not pour forth a ceaseless deluge, where the grass was not so high, so humid, so dense. I wanted to see flowers again, to walk in plains like those at Tamluk, to feel a salty breeze or the dry wind of the desert on my face. The lingering smells of putrefaction drove me almost to madness.

I was alone with three servants and the warden of the bungalow. When a stranger came to visit – a jute plantation inspector, the collector or a tea merchant *en route* for China – we would drink a glass of whisky together. I also drank alone each evening, after my bath. So tired that I barely had any sensation in my body – I could have fallen and cut myself, I would not have felt it – my nerves were none the less jangling, on edge. I shook, my breathing was tortuous and each time I got up from my chair I was overcome by dizziness. I would sit staring into space as though in a trance. All notion of time disappeared. And then I would stretch out on the chaise longue, in my only pair of pyjamas, my head lolling against my shoulder; the boy would bring a decanter of whisky and some seltzer water and I would gulp it down in small swigs. I drank until I felt a familiar warmth creep into my limbs. Then I would jump up, massage my temples, dress and go outside to walk under the rains. Breathing that air which was charged with the warm mesh of

water, I would drift into melancholia, dreaming of a simple and
happy life, of a farm near a town – a town to which I had to drive
each day! Those walks without destination were my hours of
weakness. I stayed outside until a desire to work or to sleep took
me.

I slept a lot, and heavily, especially during the three weeks
when I was working on the construction forty miles north of
Sadyia. I drove back to the bungalow late at night, sometimes
after midnight, taking the track that wound along the hillside,
trying to avoid the pot-holes; when I arrived back at the bungalow, I drank tea well-laced with rum, took some quinine and
threw myself into bed fully clothed and unwashed. We would
leave the next morning by nine o'clock.

I neglected my appearance more and more. There were very
few whites in the whole region – not one during the months of
heavy monsoon – and my only company was several Anglo-
Indian families. I would stay with them when the boredom
overwhelmed me. I liked to listen to these people speaking
English, and we drank together.

On Sundays, my servants took the train to Shillong to buy
provisions. I slept late into the morning, waking with a heavy
head and a clammy mouth. I stayed in bed all day, copying my
notes into my journal. I wanted to write a book later about the
real life of a European in Assam and I analysed myself with as
much precision as I could. My days of stagnation and depression took their place besides those other days, naturally more
numerous, when the pioneer would awake in me, full of pride
and power.

I went to Shillong only once during the whole of July. There
I treated myself to sun, a long-promised trip to the cinema, had
my gramophone repaired and bought some detective stories.
They were the only books I was capable of reading in that place.

I had been told that my work was well appreciated at headquarters – not by our agent in Shillong, an Irishman with an
inflated sense of his own importance, who had kept me waiting

outside his door without granting me an interview – but from
Narendra Sen directly. He wrote me a few typewritten lines
almost every week, full of warmth and affection.

I was due to take a month's leave in October. I was free to go
to Calcutta from the middle of August, if I had finished my
report and all my inspections and if the difficult passages
around Sadyia had been satisfactorily completed. But the
thing I dreaded most in my moments of depression occurred.
At the beginning of August I fell ill – an acute case of malaria,
complicated by nervous fatigue. One evening, I returned to the
bungalow earlier than usual. When I took a sip of my tea, I
could taste nothing. My head was turning, I was feverish and
trembling. I went to bed (having followed Harold's advice and
drunk three glasses of brandy soda) but in the morning I was
delirious. An Anglo-Indian was called, a Mr Frank: he immediately diagnosed malaria and had me taken to Sadyia that
afternoon. The sun was shining gloriously, I saw flowers,
birds. At the station, I was deeply affected by the sight of the
first white woman I had set eyes on in four months.

I remember nothing after that. I know that I was taken to
Shillong and put in the European hospital. A telegram was sent
to Calcutta and before my replacement had even arrived,
Narendra Sen had come to see me. After five days in
Shillong, I left for Calcutta in a first-class compartment,
accompanied by two Sisters of Charity and Harold. I was
admitted directly to the hospital of tropical medicine.

I opened my eyes with surprise one morning on to a white
room smelling of caramel and ammonia. In a comfortable chair
by the window, a woman was reading. For several minutes, I
listened to the whistling of the fans, trying to make out who it
was that had just said something, in a voice that was familiar to
me, about Conrad's *Lord Jim*. How much I would have given to
have been able to draw myself up in the bed and reply that the
book was mediocre and did not even begin to rival my favourite
book, *Almayers' Folly*, written in Conrad's youth.

"If you haven't read *Almayers' Folly*, you don't know Conrad's talent," I said loudly to the woman, who had gone back to her reading, her face turned towards the window.

"Good Lord! So you haven't gone deaf!" she cried out in surprise, approaching the bed.

"Do you want anything?" she asked.

"I want to shave," I said calmly, rubbing my cheeks, which felt hollow and cold beneath my rough beard.

"Would you excuse me for appearing in this negligent state? I believe I was brought here when I was delirious. I do beg you to forgive me."

She burst out laughing at that. Then, reassuming her serious tone:

"It's good that you have regained consciousness. We were beginning to give up hope. We must telephone Mr Carr. The poor boy has been asking for news of you every day."

The idea that Harold had been interested in my fate moved me so deeply that a flood of tears came to my eyes. I felt alone, abandoned and friendless among strangers, and I was frightened of dying. I pictured my death here, five weeks' journey away from my own country, and the vision paralysed me. My face froze with fear.

"What's the matter?" asked the woman, in a strange tone.

"Nothing. I want to shave," I lied.

I could not tell her the truth. She would not have understood. Tears continued to flow from my eyes.

"Do you think I will get better? That I will see New York and Paris again?" I finally murmured.

I cannot remember her reply, even though that day remains engraved in my memory. Several European doctors came, and then Harold, who sat squeezing my hand for several minutes.

"So, old chap? So, old chap?" he repeated, his eyes not leaving my face.

He had a hundred stories to amuse me with. Gertie was flirting with a manager of the Middle Bank, a very well-heeled

fellow who hardly dared kiss her and who took her to the
cinema for three rupees and eight annas a seat. Norinne, married, was growing ugly. A family of poor Anglo-Indians had
moved into my room at Wellesley Street. The young husband
brought schoolgirls back in the evening and fingered them in
his wife's presence. She, in the last month of pregnancy,
scolded him, "Jack, you'll excite yourself again."

As we were exchanging this nonsense, the engineer entered
the room. He shook my hand warmly and stroked my forehead,
looking at me intently. I introduced him to Harold.

"Delighted to meet you, Mr Sen," he said in an insolent
tone.

The engineer turned to me:

"Alain, you've been overdoing it, you've worked too hard
and now here you are ill! But don't worry, I've sorted everything out."

I felt he was uneasy in Harold's presence and that he would
have said much more to me had we been alone. He promised to
come back the following evening, after he had finished work for
the day.

"What a dreadful man!" said Harold, as soon as Mr Sen had
left. "I wonder why he's so interested in you. Maybe he wants
you to marry his daughter!"

"You're ridiculous, Harold," I said hypocritically, flushed
with embarrassment.

The image of Maitreyi appeared before me once more. I had
not pictured her for a long time. Yet this Maitreyi was more
vivacious, more human, with a red painted smile that was
almost mocking (indeed, it was curious that in my memory
her face and Mrs Sen's became one, and the mother's betel-
reddened lips merged with her daughter's large eyes and the
profusion of black hair gathered on the nape of her neck).

I studied that mental image for several moments, torn
between admiration and sadness, a mild sadness that was perhaps regret that I could not see Maitreyi in reality and also fear

that I would indeed have to see – and speak – to her again soon. Harold's presence suddenly seemed to me as displeasing and scandalous as a blasphemy. I did not understand this bizarre impression. It was certainly not a question of any love or respect that I had for Maitreyi – I took her for a vain Bengali, odd, contemptuous of whites and yet drawn to them against her will.

Harold's tales no longer seemed amusing. I wanted him to leave. Too much had happened in one day, including the sudden apparition of Maitreyi in my mind, now clear of fever, an apparition which troubled me and which would, I knew, present new problems when it was transformed into a living presence.

I had never been ill before and my convalescence, which was only just beginning, was a torment. I wanted to throw off the sheets, get dressed and wander around Calcutta. I was seized with a nostalgia for the lights of the city. I wanted to go up to China Town to eat *tchiaou* – noodles cooked in oil with leeks, lobster, egg yolks and many herbs – to stop off at Firpo's on the way back and listen to its jazz with a cocktail in my hand... The insipid regime to which I was subjected disgusted me. I was not allowed to do anything, not even smoke.

I poured out my troubles the following day to Gertie and Clara, who had come to visit me, bearing chocolate, cigarettes and fruit.

"I want to get out of this place and do exactly as I please!"

Harold arrived. He had an idea: we should throw a huge party the night I got out of hospital, followed by a walk around the lakes. Gertie, anxious for details, fetched pen and paper to draw up a list of guests: not the two Simpsons – at Norinne's engagement party, Isaac had hidden himself in a corner with a bottle of neat whisky and Gerald had cadged cigarettes – we absolutely must invite Catherine, she had been very upset when she had learnt of my illness and was forever asking after me, as for the Huber brothers and the beautiful Ivy, we'd discuss them later; we knew who the other guests would be.

Listening to Gertie write down the names and decide for me, I was not sure whether I should be saddened or amused. As I watched her, my eyes continually strayed off her face to stare into the emptiness above my head.

"Mr Sen," the sister announced.

I was gripped by the helplessness that I always feel when an Indian whom I respect is put into the company of young Anglo-Indians. The two girls, curious, turned to look at the door. Narendra Sen appeared first, his mouth enlarged, as usual, by a smile. And then, hesitant, walking with light and supple movements, Maitreyi. I thought my heart would stop. I was suddenly conscious that I was unshaven and wearing borrowed pyjamas which hardly flattered me – in short, I felt ridiculous. I shook the engineer's hand as though I were in some pain, to excuse anything inappropriate I might say later and I lifted my hands to my forehead in greeting to Maitreyi. My seriousness was doubtless more than a little comic. But the pantomime was completed when I introduced Maitreyi to my friends and she turned towards them with a brisk and decided movement, shook their hands and enquired politely: "How do you do?"

"My daughter knows two formulas for polite society – this Western one she uses only in the presence of ladies," laughed the engineer, glancing at Gertie out of the corner of his eye. I was burning with discomfort. The two girls had begun to chatter to each other, even including Harold in their conversation, whilst the engineer explained something to his daughter in Bengali. Maitreyi looked around her with a lively curiosity that was constantly tinged with a suggestion of mockery. She was listening attentively to her father's serious words but I observed a tiny smile of irony hovering around her lips. Such raw sarcasm was startling in a child so candid and so easily frightened.

Almost furious at my own awkwardness, I asked myself what it was in that presence that troubled me. Maitreyi was not in the least fascinating and I could never love her. I merely chanced to see her occasionally, in futile meetings.

"When will you come to our house, Mr Alain?"

Her voice had taken on a strange timbre and my friends turned around in unison to look at her.

"As soon as I am well."

I hesitated. I did not know how to address her. 'Miss' was unsuitable. I dared not say 'Devi'. This uncertainty made me blush and I blurted out apologetically:

"I'm sorry, I haven't shaved, my room is so untidy. I haven't been feeling at all well today..."

I simulated a gesture of great fatigue, wishing they would all leave me, and a situation which I found intolerable.

"Alain," said the engineer, "I have decided to ask you to come and stay with me. It was my wife's idea. You are not used to our Indian food and if you have to stay in Calcutta, I am afraid the life here may kill you, you are so weak from your illness. And you will save a great deal of money – in a year's time, you could have enough to go and visit your family. As for us, I'm sure I hardly need tell you, your company..."

He did not finish the sentence but gave me a large, wet smile with his frog's lips. Maitreyi looked me straight in the eyes, saying nothing, asking nothing, waiting... How I regret not having noted down, after they had left, the state of complete chaos into which Narendra Sen's words had plunged me! I have only a vague memory, not only because the events are long past but also because the violence of the innumerable emotions which were later to overwhelm me has neutralised these first feelings, making them seem to me now rather hazy and banal. I can remember, however, that two voices were crying out in me, each expressing one half of my being. The first urged me to accept this new life that no white man, to my knowledge, had ever experienced at source, the life which Lucien's research had revealed to me as magical and which Maitreyi's presence would render more fascinating and mysterious than a medieval legend. That life drew me and I felt defenceless before it.

The other voice revolted against the conspiracy which my employer had secretly woven; they wanted to paralyse me with chains, to force me into an existence bound by rigorous and secret rules. My youthful pleasures were to be sacrificed, drink prohibited, visits to the cinema curtailed. I felt that each voice expressed an intimate part of myself and that it was impossible to decide. Yet I could not delay my reply, and my thanks, much longer.

"I already owe you so much, Mr Sen! And I do not want to put you to any trouble..."

I had stammered the words, looking at the two girls, who were relishing the thought of my entry into prison. They and Harold were standing by the window, the engineer and Maitreyi close to my bed.

"Don't talk nonsense," said Narendra Sen, laughing. "We have so many spare rooms downstairs, by the library. Your company will be a ferment in the civilization of my family." I was wondering if these last words were not meant to be ironic when Gertie interrupted my reflections by taking a stupid initiative. We had agreed beforehand, as a joke, that if I were in need of rescue from Narendra Sen and his beautiful daughter, she would ask me with an air of innocence: "Alain, how is your girlfriend?" I would pretend to be embarrassed, would signal her to stop, but she was to continue "Come on! Don't play the innocent. How is Norinne?" or Isabelle or Lilian – whatever name came into her head.

I had forgotten the pact but Gertie, unfortunately, had not. Turning to me, she asked, fluttering her eyelashes maliciously, "Alain, how is your girlfriend?"

The engineer's fleshy mouth fell open with stupefaction and Maitreyi turned her head softly to look at the girl. Without waiting for a reply, Gertie continued, with great enthusiasm: "Come on! Don't play the innocent! You know you'll have to ask her opinion before you move. Isn't that right, Mr Sen?"

"Most certainly," agreed the engineer, managing a grimace of a smile.

Maitreyi contemplated her with genuine amazement and then turned to look at her father.

"I have bought you something to read," he said hastily, to change the subject. "My daughter chose *Out of the East* by Lafcadio Hearn. But it is too late now for her to read to you."

"I cannot read at all, Father, my English is incomprehensible." She had taken great care to pronounce the words correctly.

"But Alain, you haven't told me about your girlfriend!" Gertie protested, disappointed with the results of her first attempt.

"Oh leave me alone! I don't have a girlfriend!" I cried, furious at my stupidity, and hers.

"He's lying," Norinne said quietly in Narendra Sen's ear, almost confidentially. "He's a great playboy!"

What a tableau! The engineer, disconcerted and bemused, looked at his daughter, while she contemplated the scene with her absent, inhuman eyes. Harold, believing the battle won, gave me a sign of victory from the window. The whole thing seemed to me the height of absurdity and since I am incapable of taking a decision in ridiculous situations, but can only wait for some miracle to resolve the affair, I said nothing, gazing fixedly ahead, rubbing my forehead and feigning great pain.

"We should leave Alain to rest," Mr Sen declared, grasping my hand.

"We're leaving now, too," said Harold, proffering his hand to the engineer. He did not seem to know how to take leave of Maitreyi.

As soon as my visitors had left, my friends gathered around the bed, doubled up with laughter. With heavy irony, they congratulated me on Narendra Sen's invitation.

"So, Alain! That's you lost, my boy," said Gertie.

"But she isn't ugly at all!" said Clara. "Only, she seems dirty, like all the negroes. What on earth does she put in her hair?"

At a stroke, my cowardice took over. I began to mock Narendra Sen and Maitreyi with them – without believing a single word of it – and I listened with pleasure to my friends' malice. Every last trace of fascination or respect had evaporated in me.

"Come on! Let's look at the list again!" cried Gertie, bringing us back to the planned party. "I think we should invite the Huber boys – David has a car. By the way, what did you think of my presence of mind when I asked you about your girlfriend? I saved you, Alain...."

IV

Each morning I awoke with renewed astonishment. My folding bed was placed next to the door and when I opened my eyes it was to discover a strange room with a high, barred window, green-painted walls, an enormous wicker chair, two stools near a desk, several engravings nailed to the wall next to the bookcase. It always took me some minutes to gather my thoughts, to grasp where I was and to interpret the muffled sounds that came through the open window or the corridor outside the large door, which I closed at night with a wooden bar. I would part the soft mosquito-net that surrounded my bed and go out into the courtyard to wash; in the middle was a steel hut covered by a cement tank, into which the servants poured buckets of water every night. This makeshift shower was not lacking in either novelty or charm. I would fill a pitcher and empty it over myself, shivering from head to foot; it was winter and the flagstones of the courtyard were icy cold. I was proud of my courage. The others always brought a bucket of warm water with them and when they discovered that I always used the water from the tank, they could not hide their surprise and admiration. For several days the household talked of nothing but my cold morning bath. I waited for Maitreyi to compliment me in her turn. I saw her very early each morning, wearing a simple white sari, her feet bare.

One day at breakfast she spoke to me directly for the first time since I had arrived in the house.

"In your country it must be very cold. That is why all of you are white..."

As she said the word 'white', her voice took on an inflection of envy and melancholy and her gaze fell for a few moments on my partly uncovered arm, which was resting on the table. I was surprised and enchanted to discover this jealousy, but I was unable to prolong our conversation. Maitreyi drank her tea and listened; whenever I turned towards her, she would only nod in agreement.

We hardly ever spoke together. I caught glimpses of her in the corridor, I heard her singing, I knew that she spent much of the day in her room or on the terrace – and I was intrigued by this creature who seemed both so near and so distant.

I had the impression that I was constantly observed, not from suspicion but from fear that I might not be comfortable in my new surroundings. When I was alone in my room, able to laugh at the things I found strange and incomprehensible, I was sent a constant stream of cakes and fruit, tea and carefully prepared coconuts. These offerings were brought by a servant who was naked to the waist, revealing the thick growth of hair on his chest. Only with him did I dare try out my Hindustani. I would watch him as he sat outside my door, cross-legged and motionless, staring at my belongings with avid curiosity. Then, returning my gaze as I sat at my desk, he would fire a battery of questions at me. Was my bed comfortable enough? Did the mosquito net protect me? Did I like the fresh milk? Did I have brothers and sisters? Was I homesick? And I knew that in a room on the floor above, Mrs Sen and women whom I had never met were waiting for a verbatim report of my answers.

Maitreyi seemed proud and aloof. At meal-times I often caught on her lips a smile that was distant and malicious. She always left the table first, to go and chew pan in the next room, where I would hear her bursting into peals of laughter and talking Bengali. When we were with others, she never spoke to me. When we were alone, it was I who dared not speak. I was frightened of violating some part of the obscure ceremonial that governs the behaviour of an Indian. I preferred to pretend that I had not seen her, and retire to my room.

I thought of her sometimes as I smoked my pipe, wondering what she thought of me or what kind of soul lay hidden behind that curious face of a thousand expressions: there were days when she was so beautiful I could not stop looking at her. Was she stupid, like all young girls, or genuinely simple, a primitive, as I imagined all Indian girls to be?

Anxious that I was letting these useless thoughts run away with me, I would tap my pipe and return to my reading. The engineer's library occupied two rooms on the ground floor, and each day I took new books back to my desk.

Once – only a few weeks after I had come to Bhowanipore – I met her on the veranda. Without thinking, I joined my palms and brought them to my forehead in greeting; I am not sure why, but it seemed idiotic to lift my topee for an Indian girl. Perhaps I was afraid of offending her by a gesture foreign to the customs of her race, or perhaps I wanted to win her confidence.

"Who has taught you our greeting?" she asked, with a smile so friendly that I was taken aback.

"You did!"

The painful scene of our meeting on the road to China Town, when our two cars had crossed, flashed into my mind. Maitreyi looked at me for an instant and her face lost its composure, as though she had been stricken by some almost animal terror. Her lips trembled. And then, without another word, she disappeared into the corridor. Completely bemused, I went back to my room. I decided to tell the engineer of the incident, to confide my bewilderment and to ask his advice.

Several days later, I was lying on my bed, having come back tired from the office, my mind empty of thoughts. There was a knock at the door.

"When will my father be back, please?" Maitreyi asked timidly, leaning against the doorpost.

I jumped up, utterly disorientated – I swear I did not know

how to behave with her – and I replied with a superfluous flood of words, not daring to ask her to come in or to sit down.

"Mama sent me to ask you something," she added, still visibly frightened but looking me straight in the eye. "You do not amuse yourself enough with us. You stay alone in your room for hours. Mama says that if you work after sunset you will fall ill."

"What else can I do?"

"If you want, come and talk with me...or go out for a walk."

"I don't have any friends," I confided to her, approaching the door. "I don't have anyone to visit. I walk enough on my way back from work."

"You had more amusements there, at Wellesley Street," she said, smiling. Then, as if she had suddenly remembered something, she made off towards the veranda.

"I will see if there are any letters."

I waited for her, propped against the door. She hummed a tuneless melody to herself, like the ones I sometimes heard coming from her room at night, as I was drifting off to sleep. I knew that she lived up there, that her windows looked out on to the path which ran across the waste ground and that her door opened on to a balcony, over which a hanging wisteria sent a shower of red petals. I often heard her singing or quarrelling with her little sister. I saw her when she went out to the balcony, to cry out sharply 'jatchhi', like a startled bird, in reply to some call from below.

She returned with the letters and stopped in front of my door. She was trying to fix a key to a corner of her sari.

"I keep the key to the letter-box," she told me proudly. "But no one writes to me," she added a little sadly, as she looked through the letters.

"Who could write to you?"

"People...what good is the mail, if it does not bring me letters from people whom I do not know?"

I looked at her, baffled. She stood immobile for a moment,

her eyes closed, as if she were being assailed by some frightening thought.

"I think I have made a grammatical mistake," she said.

"You haven't made any mistake."

"Then why do you look at me in such a way?"

"I don't understand. How can people you don't know write to you?"

"It's impossible, isn't it? Papa says the same thing. He thinks you are very intelligent. Is it true?"

I grinned idiotically and was about to attempt a joke when she continued:

"Would you like to see the terrace?"

I accepted joyfully. I longed to lie out on the roof of the house in the heat of the sun, to contemplate the garden, to look down at the parks and the villas of the district through which, at first, I had regularly lost my way when I returned to the house in the evenings.

"Can I go as I am?"

She looked at me with surprise.

"I'm wearing tennis shoes and no socks. I don't have a tie or a jacket."

She continued staring at me and then asked suddenly, in a strange tone of curiosity:

"How do people go up to the roof in your country?"

"We don't have flat roofs."

"No terraces? None at all?"

"None at all."

"That must be sad. How do you look at the sun, then?"

"In the street, outside, anywhere."

She reflected for an instant.

"That is why you are white. It is very beautiful. I also would like to be white. Is it possible, do you think?"

"I don't know, but I suspect not. Perhaps with powder..."

"Powder washes off. Did you have powder put on your face, when you were a child?"

"No. We don't do that."

Her face lit up.

"If you had been powdered, you would have fallen ill. Tolstoy said so."

Astonished anew, I must have looked at her with an expression of amusement, for her own expression changed abruptly and she said, with great seriousness:

"You do not know Count Leo Tolstoy, the great Russian writer? He writes very well. He was rich but when he was old he gave everything up and retired into the forest. Like an Indian."

She remembered the terrace then, and asked me to follow her.

We climbed the staircase together. I was somewhat uneasy as we passed the women's room, but she spoke deliberately loudly so that her mother would hear us and would know – as Maitreyi declared to me later – that I was 'amusing myself'. Apparently, my hostess had not slept for several nights, for worry that I might be getting bored without 'distractions' – music, friends, gramophone.... As I stepped out on to the terrace, I was suddenly overwhelmed by a joy that was almost euphoria. I did not know that the world seen from the top of a house could appear so different; the town was calmer, the surroundings greener. I walked through the avenue of trees in Bhowanipore every day, but I had never noticed there were so many.

Leaning against the walled edge, I looked down into the courtyard. I remembered the day I had seen Maitreyi stretched out on the steps, laughing – a day which had seemed to last for several years. Years had also passed since Maitreyi had come to ask me nervously, "When will my father be back, please?"...

I did not understand her. She seemed a child, a primitive. Her words drew me, her incoherent thinking and her naïveté enchanted me. For a long time, I was to flatter myself by thinking of our relationship as that of civilized man and barbarian.

She had brought little Chabu up on to the terrace.

"My sister does not speak English," she said to me, "but she understands it. She wants you to tell her a story. I also like stories."

Once again, I felt awkward and passive in the presence of the two girls, who stood in front of me, holding hands, under a sky of approaching dusk that was more beautiful than any I had ever seen. I had the bizarre impression of dreaming, of watching the scene changing shape before my eyes. Somewhere a curtain had lifted... or perhaps it was I who had changed... I do not know any more. "It's a long time since I read any stories," I replied, at last, "and then, there's a problem. I can't tell stories. It takes a gift. Not everyone has it."

At that, the girls' faces fell, but it was with a sadness so spontaneous and so candid that I felt guilty and tried to remember one of the fables I had read in my childhood. None came to me. The knowledge of my own blankness paralysed me. I quickly ran through stories by Perrault, Grimm, Andersen and Lafcadio Hearn in my head. They all seemed too banal. If I were to tell them *Little Red Riding Hood*, *Sleeping Beauty* or *The Enchanted Treasure*, I would surely appear ridiculous. I wanted to recount a marvellous tale, full of adventure and complexity, one that even Maitreyi would enjoy. A tale, in short, worthy of an intelligent and cultivated young man: original, memorable, symbolic. Nothing of the sort came to my mind.

"Tell us a story with a tree," said Chabu, looking at her sister to make sure she had expressed herself correctly.

I thought I might manage to improvise something or other and began wildly: "Once upon a time, there was a tree, and at the root of the tree there lay a hidden treasure. A knight..."

"What is a knight?" asked Chabu.

Her sister explained to her in Bengali, as I tried to think what I could say next.

"One night, the knight dreamed that a fairy was showing him where the treasure was hidden..."

I was ashamed of these imbecilities and, not daring to look at the girls, I applied myself to tying my shoe-laces.

"With the help of an enchanted mirror, the knight found the treasure..."

I could not go on, and was certain that Maitreyi must be sharing my embarrassment. Yet when I lifted my eyes, I saw that she was listening with rapt attention and seemed curious to know what would happen next.

"But what was the knight's amazement when he discovered underneath the treasure a live dragon, with blazing eyes, breathing fire..."

I blushed as I spoke these last words.

"Then..."

"But the tree," interrupted Chabu, "what did the tree say?"

I was at a loss to answer and said to myself: pantheism!

"Well, the story is like that. Not every tree has a soul. Only magic trees have one."

Chabu turned to Maitreyi and said something with great fervour. For the first time I was truly sorry not to understand their language. The rhythms were very gentle, like those of Italian, the vowels very long. One had the impression that the sentence was going to fly off at any moment into a song.

"What does she want to know?"

"She asks if her tree has a soul. I told her that all trees have souls."

"She has a tree?"

"It is not a tree, exactly. It's the shrub in the courtyard, the one whose branches grow against the veranda. Chabu feeds it every day with biscuits and cakes."

I repeated happily to myself: pantheism, pantheism! What rare documents I had before me!

"That's nice, Chabu. But your tree does not eat biscuits."

"But I eat them!" she cried, very surprised at my comment.

I could not lose such a discovery. On the pretext that I

wanted to smoke my pipe, I went back to my room. I shuttered the door with the wooden bar and wrote in my journal: "First discussion with Maitreyi. The primitive nature of her thinking to be noted. A child who has read too much. Today on the terrace, painful episode with my story. I am incapable of telling stories, no doubt because of my discomfort with all that is innocent and naïve. A revelation: Chabu, a pantheistic soul. She makes no distinction between her own feelings and those of inanimate objects. For example, she gives biscuits to a tree because she eats biscuits herself, even though she knows the tree cannot eat them. Very interesting."

Having consigned these thoughts to paper, I stretched myself out on the bed, abandoning myself to the free run of my thoughts. I do not know what doubts then assailed me but after a few moments I got up, opened my journal again and wrote: "Perhaps I am wrong."

That evening, I worked with Narendra Sen in his study. As I was leaving, he put his hand on my shoulder and said:"My wife cares for you very much, Alain. I want you to feel at home here. You can move freely about the house, go into all the rooms. We are not orthodox and we do not keep purdah. If you need anything, please tell my wife or Maitreyi – I believe you two are quite good friends?"

I felt that the day's events entitled me to agree. However, I decided to confide my small difficulties to him.

"Every Indian girl behaves in that way with a stranger," he laughed.

He then told me of an incident that had occurred the year before. They had gone to have tea at the Italian consulate. It was raining. There was only one umbrella and, as the consul helped her across the inner courtyard, he had taken Maitreyi's arm. Such a gesture from a stranger had terrified her so much that she had run off into the street, in the rain, and jumped into the motor-car. She had stopped crying only when they had reached Bhowanipore, where she had thrown herself into the refuge of her mother's arms. Maitreyi had been almost fifteen at the time.

On another occasion, a European family had invited her into their box at the theatre. In the darkness, a dandy had tried to take her hand. She had whispered to him, loud enough for all her neighbours to hear: "I will hit you on the face with my slipper!" Scandal. The whole box gets up. Mrs X (she is too well-known in Calcutta for me to mention her name) tries to intervene. "Have I made a grammatical mistake?" asks Maitreyi.

I laughed at the story but I wondered if she were truly such an innocent; was she not hiding some finely cultivated sense of humour, amusing herself at our expense? This doubt haunted me afterwards, every time I heard Maitreyi talking loudly or laughing uproariously in a neighbouring room.

"Did you know that she writes poetry?"

"I thought it quite likely."

The revelation did not endear Maitreyi to me. Every promising young girl writes poetry – and Mr Sen, as I noted with some distaste, took his daughter, with complete confidence, to be a prodigy. He had often declared to me that she was a genius and as a result, I thought she must be quite stupid – although it was true that she had already passed her school matriculation and was now studying for a Bachelor of Arts at the university. Her vanity no longer surprised me.

"Yes, she writes philosophical poems which Tagore likes very much," he added, looking at me out of the corner of his eye.

"Really?" I replied, indifferent.

As I was going downstairs, I met Maitreyi coming out of the library, a book under her arm.

"I didn't know you were a poet!" I said to her, in a tone of some irony.

She blushed and backed against the wall. This insane sensitivity was beginning to exasperate me.

"Really, there's no harm in writing poems! The important thing is that they are beautiful."

"Who told you that mine are not beautiful?"

"I don't doubt their beauty. I simply wonder if you have enough experience of life to write philosophical poems."

She reflected for an instant and then burst out laughing. The peals of her laughter became more and more open and sincere and she crossed her arms over her breasts in a curious gesture of modesty.

"Why are you laughing?"

She stopped abruptly.

"I should not laugh?"

"I don't know. I don't understand at all. People must do as they wish, after all. I thought you would be able to say why you were laughing..."

"Papa thinks you are very intelligent."

I shrugged impatiently.

"That is why you always ask questions. I am afraid to make mistakes, to make you angry."

Her face took on an expression that made me suddenly happy.

"And why are you afraid to make me angry?"

"Because you are our guest. A guest is sent by God..."

"And if the guest is a wicked man?"

I was interrogating her as one would a child, although her expression had become serious – savage, even.

"God calls him back."

"Which god?"

"His god."

"What? Every man has his own god?"

I had stressed these last words. She looked at me, reflected, closed her eyes, and when she opened them they were full of tenderness and affection; I had not seen such an expression in them before.

"I am wrong, no?"

"How can I say? I am not a philosopher."

"I am a philosopher," she said at once, looking at me intently. "I like to dream, to think and to write poetry."

And so that is philosophy, I thought, and I smiled.

"I would like to be old, like Robi Thakkur."

"Who is Robi Thakkur?"

I was disturbed, in a way that perplexed me, by the tone of her voice, now warmer, and heavy with sorrow.

"Tagore. I would like to be as old as he. When one is old, one loves more and suffers less."

She blushed at her words and made as if to leave. But she controlled herself and stopped; she had glanced at me and no doubt understood how awkward I felt, standing there in front of her against the balustrade, uncertain of what to do. She changed the subject.

"Mama is very worried. You have got thinner. She read in a book that at home Europeans have soup every day. You have never had soup with us. Here, we do not keep stock, we give it to the hens."

"But I don't like soup," I told her, to reassure her.

"That is a great pity!"

"But how does it matter?"

"Because of Mama."

She was going to add something but changed her mind; I was embarrassed by this sudden silence and did not know how to interpret the glint of anger that had momentarily flashed in her eyes. I thought I must have offended her.

"Please forgive me, if I have committed some fault. I do not know how to behave with Indians."

She had gone towards the staircase, but stopped suddenly when she heard those words. She looked at me once more, a strange look – I am incapable of describing those looks or the continual changes in her expression – and I stood immobile, stupefied, staring back at her helplessly.

"Why do you ask my forgiveness? Why do you want to make me suffer?"

"I don't have the least intention of doing that," I said, utterly confused. "I thought I had offended you and so..."

"How can a man ask forgiveness of a girl?"

"When he has committed some fault...well, it's a custom."

"To a girl?"

"And even to a child!"

"Do all Europeans behave like this?"

I hesitated.

"True Europeans, yes..."

She closed her eyes for a second, reflecting, and then burst out laughing, again crossing her arms over her breasts in a gesture of fear.

"Perhaps white people ask each other forgiveness. But me?"

"Of course!"

"And Chabu?"

"Her too."

"Chabu is darker than me."

"That's not true."

Her eyes glinted.

"Yes it is! Mama and I are paler than Chabu and Papa. Have you not noticed?"

"Perhaps, but what difference does it make?"

"You do not think it is important? It will be more difficult for Chabu to marry because she is darker. Her dowry will have to be much larger..."

She blushed at these words and looked embarrassed; I myself was rather uncomfortable. After Lucien's visit, I had researched the subject of Hindu marriage and I knew how painful it was for a girl to speak of this system of barter. Fortunately for us both, Mrs Sen called for her at that moment and she ran off thankfully, her book under her arm, crying "Jatchhi!"

I returned to my room, delighted at the day's discoveries. I would soon be called for dinner, and I washed quickly. As was the Bengal custom, we dined very late in the evening – between ten and eleven o'clock – before retiring to bed.

I opened my diary to add several notes. I hesitated for several seconds, my pen poised, and then I closed the book. "Idiocies", I thought.

V

I want to make it absolutely clear, straight away, that I never once thought of love during the first few months of my stay in that house. Rather, I was fascinated by Maitreyi's character, bewitched by the mystery that seemed to envelop her. I thought about her, noted down a great many of her words and actions in my diary, was troubled and intrigued by the strange, unfathomable charm of her eyes, her responses, her laugh. It is quite true that I was attracted to the girl. Even her walk possessed some power that pulled and enchanted. But it is also true that the whole of my existence at Bhowanipore, not just Maitreyi, was miraculous and unreal to me. My coming to the house had been so quick, so effortless, and my life there was still so mysterious and disquieting that I sometimes had to shake myself awake from that Indian dream and remember my real life, my European life... And then I would smile. What a transformation! Almost nothing of my old world now interested me. I saw no one, other than guests of the Sen family. Mathematical physics no longer attracted me. Instead, I threw myself into novels, essays on political economy and, above all, history.

One day Maitreyi asked if I would like to learn Bengali: she would be my teacher. I already possessed a simple primer, which I had bought during my first week at the house and which I consulted when I was alone to find out what it was that Maitreyi cried out when she was called or when she was annoyed. I knew that "jatcchi" meant "I'm coming" and that the words I heard so often, "ki vishan" meant "how extraordinary". My little book was barely more informative and I accepted Maitreyi's offer of lessons. In exchange, I would teach her French.

We had our first lesson that morning, and from then on held them directly after breakfast, in my room. I had suggested the library at first, but the engineer himself insisted that we work in my room, where it would be quieter. These obvious attempts to bind us in friendship – and his wife's excessive tolerance of them – began to disconcert me more and more and then to make me suspicious. At times, I wondered if my hosts were not hoping to marry me to Maitreyi. Yet such a project was surely impossible: they would have lost everything – their caste, their reputation.

We seated ourselves at the table – I took care that I was not too close to Maitreyi – and the lesson began. I realized at once that I would never learn by this method; she explained any difficulties to me so kindly, she shifted her chair towards mine and looked at me with such intensity that I took nothing in. Occasionally I muttered, "Oh, yes," and went on watching her, lost in that gaze, in the pleasure of that fluid expansion of the senses which emanates from the eyes yet which has little to do with sight. I had never known a face that waged a fiercer battle against conventional beauty. I have kept three photographs of Maitreyi; I cannot recognize her in any of them.

The French lesson would then follow. I was just beginning to teach her the alphabet and the system of pronouns when she interrupted me.

"How do you say 'I am a young girl'?"

I told her. She repeated joyfully, "Je suis une jeune fille. Je suis une jeune fille."

Her pronunciation was astonishingly accurate, but she did not benefit from my work; she interrupted continually to ask what the French was for a succession of words and phrases, without rhyme or reason.

"Say something. You translate and I will repeat," she proposed, as though she had discovered an excellent method.

A curious conversation began, Maitreyi asking after each new phrase whether I was translating correctly.

"In your place, I would translate something else," she declared.

After a few of these sessions, she stopped looking at me and took to amusing herself while I talked. She would scribble in her notebook, over and over, "Robi Thakkur, Robi Thakkur", sign her name, draw flowers, in painstaking calligraphy write "Calcutta", "I regret" or "Why?" and compose little verses in Bengali. Unable to look her in the eyes, I had the disagreeable impression that I was speaking to a stranger. Yet I dared not ask her to stop.

"You do not like me to write while you talk to me? Why do you not tell me so?" she asked one day, looking at me directly and giving her voice a feminine inflection that took me by surprise.

I hastily muttered something and went on with the lesson, disconcerted and not a little angry. She looked down at her book again. I could not stop myself from glancing at it. She had written "It is late, it is too late, but it is not very late."

"What does that mean?" I asked.

"I am just amusing myself," she replied, and began to erase the inscription letter by letter, drawing a flower over each one.

"I have just had an idea. I will give French lessons to Chabu."

I remember that I burst out into a fit of laughter at that; she too began to laugh.

"You think I could not? I would be a better teacher than you, even of French."

She spoke seriously, but her voice rang with humour, and she darted a little sideways glance at me.

She had never before acted like this, and a quiver of joy went through me. Now she was more of a woman and somehow more mine. I understood her when she played the coquette, far more than when she seemed an unfathomable barbarian, a 'pantheist' as one part of me called her.

I do not know what I replied in French – it was only some triviality – but I refused to translate. She grew animated and flushed, asked me to repeat the phrase word for word and then began leafing through the French-English dictionary to discover the meaning of my mysterious declaration. She could not decipher any of it and became irritated.

"You do not know how to amuse yourself!"

"I do not care to amuse myself while I am giving a lesson."

I had assumed an air of great severity. She closed her eyes, as was her custom when she was reflecting. Her eyelids were a shade paler than the rest of her face and they were lined now with a faint purple shadow that was very lovely. Then, brusquely, she stood up.

"I will see if the post has arrived."

I waited. I was angry that she was not learning anything, and worried that her father would hold me responsible for her ignorance.

She returned almost at once, looking subdued. She was holding two sprigs of wisteria that she had picked from the veranda.

"Shall we continue the lesson? Je suis une jeune fille."

"Very good, that's one phrase you know. And now?"

"J'apprends le français."

"Oh really! We learnt that last week!"

"The girl in the motor-car, did you teach her French?" she asked, point blank, looking me straight in the eyes but with a slight expression of fear on her face. I reddened.

"No, of course not! She is much too stupid. Even if I spent five years trying to teach her, it would do no good..."

"How old will you be in five years?"

"Between thirty and thirty-one."

"Not even half his age!" she murmured, as though to herself.

She leaned over her book and began to write "Robi Thakkur" in Bengali characters, then in European. I was irritated. Her passion for an old man of seventy unnerved me. And then I had hoped, fleetingly, that the mention of Gertie would awaken a hint of jealousy in her, but she had already forgotten... I was beginning to suspect that my pupil was mocking me, pretending to a naïveté she did not possess. I would never have admitted that I was being hoodwinked by a child of sixteen who inspired no feeling of love in me – it was merely intellectual delight that I experienced in her presence. I saw now that I had wrongly interpreted all the clever, subtle moves by which she had doubtless wanted to catch me out, to make me look ridiculous. I was, after all, the first young man that Maitreyi had known at close quarters. I was living in the same house, I was white... there was no lack of reasons for her to seduce me. This thought filled me with exhilaration and I knew, with great self-satisfaction, that I was now immunised against her. I would be able to rise above these games, let myself become the object of the passion which I had inspired in her, remaining for my own part quite detached. My diary of that time bears witness to this state of mind. I observed Maitreyi's little ploys with calm lucidity. She had thrown off her initial shyness with me and had begun to talk quite freely; she gave me the constant impression that she was acting a part in some play.

She stood up, arranged her books and took one of the wisteria sprigs from the table.

"I chose the reddest..."

She made as if to leave.

"Take them both," I said, pointing to the flower she had left. I began filling my pipe nonchalantly, to show her just how little I cared about her wisteria.

She came back, took it, thanked me for the lesson and left. But on the threshold she turned around abruptly and threw one of the flowers on to my desk – she had put the other in her hair – and then disappeared. I heard her running up the stairs two at a time.

What was I to make of this? A declaration of love? I opened my diary and noted the incident, adding a stupid commentary.

At breakfast the following morning, Maitreyi asked me casually what I had done with the flower.

"I'm drying it."

I was lying – I no longer had it – but I wanted her to suspect that some romantic attachment was beginning to form in my heart.

"I lost mine on the stairs," she confessed sadly.

I reflected on the incident all day and dreamt of absurd possibilities. Back in my room that evening, I studied myself in the mirror. For the first time in my life, I regretted that I was not more handsome. Yet deep down inside me, there is an unquenchable fund of humour and I burst into laughter when I realized what I was doing: standing in front of a mirror pulling faces at myself as if I were a film actor. I threw myself on to the bed, happy in the knowledge that I was intelligent and lucid... At that moment, Maitreyi appeared with her books.

"Do we have a lesson today?" she asked nervously.

We began with Bengali. I was making rapid progress; I studied alone each evening and often practised with Chabu. Maitreyi gave me a text to translate. Whilst I was writing, she asked:

"Where did you put the flower?"

"It is being pressed."

"Show it to me."

"I cannot," I said, in a tone of great mystery.

"Have you hidden it in a secret place?"

She seemed utterly captivated and I said no more, leaving her to her illusions. We finished the lesson and when she had gone, I went out to the veranda, broke off a flower which looked similar to the one she had given me, dried it a little with the ash from my pipe and then pressed it. One would have thought it had been picked long before.

I saw Maitreyi again at dinner. Her eyes were shining with a strange light and she laughed incessantly.

"Mama says we are being foolish!"

Frozen with horror, I looked at her and then at Mrs Sen, who was smiling benevolently. The idea that they were actually encouraging our sentimental games made me feel quite ill. It was as though a plot were being hatched against me: I was meant to fall in love with Maitreyi. That was why we were always left alone together, why the engineer was always retiring to his room to read a detective story, why none of the women who lived on that floor ever came to spy on us. I felt an intense desire to leave, then and there. Nothing revolts me so much as such machinations. I kept my eyes lowered and ate in silence. We were alone: the engineer was dining with friends. Maitreyi talked incessantly. I had already noticed that she was silent only in the presence of her father or of a stranger. With the rest of the household, she was positively garrulous.

"You should walk a little, at night," she said to me, "Mama thinks you are too thin."

I replied in a tone of disdain, which Mrs Sen seemed instantly to notice. She said something to her daughter in Bengali. Maitreyi responded sulkily and tapped her foot against the table leg. I carried on eating as though I were quite unconscious of all this, but the knowledge that I had upset Mrs Sen pained me. She was almost like a mother to me, even though she seemed so young, so fearful. When I took leave of them, Maitreyi followed me into the corridor. She had never come so near my room at night.

"Please, give to me that flower!"

I saw she was genuinely disturbed: she had even made a careless mistake in her English. I dared not ask her to come into my room. It was she who, without waiting or asking, crossed the threshold. I showed her the dried flower.

"Here it is...but leave it with me, I would like to keep it."

Perhaps I said something else – it was in any case some clumsy attempt at mystery and sentimentality.

She took the flower in her trembling hand, examined it and

then began laughing so hard that she had to lean against the door. "This is not it," she cried.

I must have paled slightly, for she shot me a look of triumph. I feigned indignation.

"How can you say such a thing?"

"The other had one of my hairs in its petals..."

She looked at me once more, highly amused, and then left. Late into the night, I heard her singing in her room.

VI

One morning, Narendra Sen came and knocked on my door. He was going into town with Maitreyi, who was wearing her most beautiful sari, made of a deep, glossy brown silk, a matching shawl and golden slippers.

"She is giving a talk on the essence of beauty," announced the engineer.

I looked at them both, stunned, and gave her what I hoped was an admiring smile. Maitreyi played with her shawl, indifferent. In her hand, she had a scroll of paper, her manuscript. Her hair had been dressed with great care and she must have used a profusion of Keora Attar on it, for the disturbing fragrance filled my room.

"I sincerely wish her great success. As long as she is not shy!" I added, looking at her.

"It is not the first time she will speak in public," replied Narendra Sen, with a touch of arrogance.

"It is a shame you do not understand Bengali very well. You could have come to listen to her."

I returned to my room, more than a little disquieted and filled with a lingering doubt. I had to force myself to concentrate on my reading. The image of Maitreyi discoursing on beauty haunted me. It must be a joke, I said to myself, or else I have been an insensitive brute. I would never have dreamed that the child could dissect such a serious question. The phrase ran senselessly through my head – the essence of beauty, the essence of beauty.

Two hours later, I heard the car pull up in front of the house and I went out to the veranda to greet them. Maitreyi seemed a little sad.

"How did it go?"

"They did not understand it all. She was too profound. She dealt with ideas that were too intimate – creation and emotion, the interiorization of the beautiful. The public did not always follow..."

I thought that Maitreyi would stop and talk to me, but she passed my door and ran upstairs. I heard her closing her windows. I was utterly restless, I wanted to go out, to walk in the park.

I was walking down the veranda steps when a voice suddenly called from on high:

"Where are you going?"

Maitreyi was leaning over the balustrade, dressed in a plain white house sari, her hair flowing loose over her shoulders, her arms bare. I replied that I was going for a walk to buy tobacco.

"You can send a servant."

"And what about me? What can I do?"

"If you want, come up, we can talk..."

The invitation troubled me. I circulated quite freely about the house, but I had never gone into Maitreyi's room. However, I was upstairs in an instant; she was waiting for me in front of the door. Her face was tired and tinged with an expression of supplication, her lips strangely red – this last detail struck me. I learnt later that she always painted her lips with pan before going to town, according to the rites of Bengal elegance.

"Please remove your shoes."

I thought I must look ridiculous in my socks and I felt even more ill at ease. She beckoned me to sit on a cushion near the balcony door. I looked around the room. It had a monastic air. It was as large as mine, but contained only a bed, a chair and two cushions. On the balcony was a small writing desk. No pictures, cupboard or mirror.

"Chabu sleeps on the bed," she told me, smiling.

"And you?"

"On this mat."

From underneath the bed, she took out a mat woven from bamboo straws. It was as fine as a piece of cloth. I was moved. For an instant, I had the impression that I was sitting opposite a saint and I could almost have fallen on my knees before her. But suddenly she laughed and the moment had passed.

"Often, I sleep on the balcony. The breeze blows over me and I can hear the noise from the street."

It was a corner of the park rather than a real street; no one passed at night.

"I like to listen to it," she said, leaning out over the window ledge.

"That path – who knows where it leads?"

"To Clive Street," I replied jokingly.

"And Clive Street?"

"To the Ganges."

"And then?"

"To the sea."

She trembled and moved closer to me.

"When I was very small, smaller than Chabu, we went every year to Puri, by the sea. Grandfather had a hotel there. Nowhere else has waves like those at Puri, I am sure. They were as big as this house."

I imagined those gigantic waves and Maitreyi beside them, lecturing on the essence of beauty. The vision made me smile.

"Why are you laughing?" she asked sadly.

"Waves as big as this house? I think you must be exaggerating..."

"And so? Is that funny? Grandfather exaggerated much more than I – he had eleven children."

She turned away from me. I thought I had offended her and murmured an apology.

"Do not trouble yourself," she said, with a cold smile.

"Before, you truly asked my forgiveness. Now you yourself do not believe your words. Do you like Swinburne?"

I was used to these abrupt changes of subject and I replied that I did indeed like Swinburne. She picked up a worn book from the little table and indicated a passage from "Anactoria" which had been underlined in pencil. I read it aloud. After several verses, she snatched the book from my hands.

"Perhaps another poet will please you. But you do not like Swinburne enough."

I was bewildered. I replied defensively that the whole of neo-Romantic poetry was not worth one of Valéry's poems and I begun a critique of the philosophical poem, that hybrid and disappointing breed. She listened attentively, studying my face intently, as she had done in our first lessons together, making small nodding movements with her head. However, I had hardly warmed to my theme when she cut me off.

"Would you like some tea?"

She went out into the corridor and cried out her orders to the kitchen below.

"I hope you are not going to spill tea over my trousers, like you did last year with Lucien!" I teased her.

She seemed about to laugh when she suddenly stopped, as though she had been petrified, in the middle of the room. She exclaimed in Bengali and disappeared. From the sound of her footsteps, I knew she had gone to her father's study next to the drawing-room.

She returned, carrying some books.

"They arrived this morning, from Paris. But I was too occupied with my lecture and I forgot them."

She held out two copies of *L'Inde avec les Anglais* by Lucien Metz. Sent by the publisher, they had not been dedicated.

"One is for you," said Maitreyi.

"Do you know what we will do? I will dedicate my copy to you and you will do the same with yours."

She clapped her hands and ran to get ink. With obvious

difficulty, she restrained her impatience as I wrote "To my friend Maitreyi Devi. A pupil and a teacher. In memory, etc." The formula "etc." intrigued her. On her copy she wrote simply: "To my friend".

"What if someone steals the book?"

"It would not matter. He also might be my friend..."

She seated herself on the matting, her chin resting against her knees, and watched me as I drank my tea. Night was falling. Outside in the street, the lamp had been lit and the shadow of the palm tree, a strange blue colour, had lengthened eerily. I wondered what the other occupants of the house could be doing, why I heard no voices or footsteps. Was there some conspiracy? Why were we always left alone, even in Maitreyi's room – sitting in the shadows, lit only by the quivering blue light of a street-lamp?

"Our friendship begins today, doesn't it?" she asked me very softly, as she took my empty cup.

"Why today? We have been friends for a long time, since our first serious conversation..."

She sat down again on her bamboo mat and declared that if we had truly been friends she would have confided her sadness to me. I begged her to tell me everything but she said nothing, keeping her eyes on my face. I too remained silent.

"Robi Thakkur did not come to my lecture today," she said at last.

I was pained by this declaration. I wanted to insult her, tell her that she was mistaken if she took me for a friend, that her passion was ridiculous...

"You love him," I said, maliciously.

I was about to go on in this vein, to anger her, but she turned to me brusquely and asked sharply:

"Do you find it agreeable to sit in the dark with young girls?"

"It's the first time I've done it," I replied, at random.

She lay down on the mat.

"I would like to be alone," she said. She seemed exhausted, crushed.

I left, putting my shoes on with difficulty in the dark. I went downstairs on tiptoe, filled with a curious anger that was close to fury. When I got to my room, I saw with frustration that all the lamps had been lit.

Extracts from my diary:
Her beauty is not conventional, it does not meet classic dictates. Her face is rebelliously expressive. She enchants in the magical sense of the word. I have to confess that I thought of her all night. And even now, instead of working, I visualize her, a pale silhouette in a sari of blue silk, all interwoven with gold thread. And her hair! The Persians were right, in their poetry, to compare women's hair to snakes. What will happen? I do not know. Probably I will forget her.

Oh God, when will I find peace?

Chabu wrote a story and Maitreyi translated it for me on the terrace today, laughing all the time. A king had a son named Phool, who rode out one day into a huge forest. Suddenly, everything in the forest turned into flowers: only prince and horse remained prince and horse... When he returned to the palace, Phool told his father of the marvel, but his father did not believe him and scolded him for telling lies. He called the royal pandit and ordered him to read moral precepts against lying to his son. However, the prince still insisted that he had spoken the truth. So the king assembled his army and set off for the forest. No sooner had they entered it than they all turned into flowers. A day passed. Then Phool went to the forest, with the books containing the moral tales and the precepts against lying. He tore out the pages and threw them to the four winds. As the paper scattered, the king's soldiers were turned back into humans and then, last of all, the king...

I am beginning to notice unpleasant traits in Mr Sen. He is swollen with arrogance and takes himself for a remarkable and superior being. Tonight on the terrace he asked me, in a round-about way, about the prostitutes in Paris: he wants to go there for several months to have his high blood pressure treated. He also suffers from intermittent eye trouble, he sees "moving flies".

The engineer's cousin, Mantu, has arrived from Delhi. He has the room next to mine. He is thirty or so, small and slight, a schoolmaster who has just taken up a post at the Government Commercial School. Almost at once, we became good friends. He told me that he had changed his job so as to get married here in Calcutta. He himself does not want the marriage but Narendra Sen is very keen. Mantu has the foreboding of catastrophe. He is frightened.

Mantu is a wonderful fellow. When he speaks English, he closes his eyes. He laughs a lot. His marriage ceremony began four days ago and finished this evening. We celebrated at the bride's house (she is called Lilu, is dark, a simple country girl, but very pleasant) and at the engineer's. I have been observing Narendra Sen's attitude to this marriage: it is he who had organized the whole thing and yet he has just complained to me about the haste with which Mantu 'suggests' and decides. Mantu venerates Sen so much that he has offered him his bride's virginity. In certain regions of India, it is the custom for the disciple to offer 'prima nox' to his guru (Mantu has often told me that he considers the engineer not only a cousin but also a guru).

I saw everything in detail. At every moment, I was at the centre of everything. I was wearing an Indian tunic and trousers, made of silk, and I have to say that they suited me to perfection. My wearing of this costume, the unforced interest which I had in the ceremony, my efforts to speak only in Bengali, all won me a genuine popularity. Indian society enchants me; the friendship of an Indian is of inestimable value.

I am sometimes seized by a strange feeling of love, in the divine sense that the word has here, and look on every woman as a mother. I have never felt a filial devotion so pure and so soothing as I feel towards Mrs Sen. Everyone calls her 'Mama' as a matter of course. When I catch sight in the street of a blue sari like the one she wears, I do not even have to see the woman's face to be filled with the same emotion: I am a son, I need to be caressed and only in India can I find a maternal passion as selfless, as noble, as pure. During the ceremony, I took off into agreeable flights of fancy, imagining myself married to Maitreyi. Truth be told – I was happy. I dreamed of her all through the wedding. Fiancée, lover... But I never lost my head. I tried to persuade myself that she is not so beautiful, I thought of her hips, which are too large for her waist. I thought that by seeing all kinds of imperfections in her, I would distance her from me – in fact, as often happens, the imperfections somehow only served to bring her closer to me.

I do not know whether the insinuations which the family make are simply pleasantries or whether they are based on a serious plan of marriage, devised by Narendra Sen himself. One night at dinner, Mrs Sen made a remark that seemed to hint at this plan of her husband's.

It is impossible to go on thinking of a conspiracy. They consider marriage a joy and a duty, they sincerely like me, and then Maitreyi is so well-regarded in Bengal society that she could easily find a better match than me.

I wonder what would become of me if I loved Maitreyi? Is it possible that I could lose all my lucidity and, caught in the trap, accept? She is without question the most gifted and enigmatic of all the girls I have known. But obviously I cannot marry. What would become of my freedom? Goodbye to journeys in extraordinary countries and goodbye to my daily adventures!

How happy I am for the moment! And what enchantment.

Last night, in the bridal chamber, amid a sea of flowers, the girls sang and Maitreyi read a poem "composed especially for the occasion".

A reaction which has been nagging at me for the last few days: if I understand them to be hinting at my eventual marriage, if I simply suspect it, I am gripped by an instant and brutal agitation.

My senses overwhelm me, my prolonged self-restraint excites my nervous system and I become upset and disturbed. I am afraid of the destiny that is shaping itself. I am both afraid and exultant; I am in love with danger. I dare not openly declare that I will never marry. Neither can I leave. That would be stupid. And I remain an irreproachably moral creature, even though the devil inside tells me I am nothing of the sort...

Today Mantu told the women something I had recently confided to him: that I do not wish to marry and never will. Maitreyi now seems angry and contemptuous towards me. She has not come for our lessons. She doesn't stop to talk any more when I come back from work. Mrs Sen is no longer affectionate.

This change disconcerts me. Yet it is what I had wanted. I was so frightened of this love that I suspected all kinds of secret plots and intentions.

Tonight I heard Maitreyi screaming with laughter at some joke that Khokha made (a young man, a poor relation who has come to take advantage of the hospitality during the wedding feast. His room is off the corridor). I was writing in my room. My heart tightened with a painful knot of jealousy. How pathetic I have become!

While I felt around me the warmth and affection of the whole family, Maitreyi inspired nothing but indifference in me. I was frightened when I sensed a matrimonial trap. But here I am, my vocation as a bachelor finally declared and Maitreyi has changed; it is I who am beginning to love her. I am jealous. I dread my destiny. This solitude is painful.

What a change! Now I take my meals alone with the engineer and Mantu. The women eat afterwards. Without Maitreyi, all joy has left the table. I want to leave on a tour of inspection in south Bengal. When I come back, I will find some pretext to leave the house. The experiment is coming to an end. It has already lasted too long.

It has been raining for two days, the sky is dark. Today water is coming down in torrents. I went out on to the veranda to look at the flooded streets. Maitreyi, dressed magnificently in pink velvet and black silk, was also there. I know that she writes poetry about rain and perhaps she was composing a poem today, upstairs in her room. We addressed a few cold words to each other. She seemed indifferent and distracted. Could I have believed her so rich in womanly experience that she is capable of judging with such precision the attitudes this new situation demands?

It is as though I am a stranger in this house, where I have known the most sincere affection, the most authentic Indian hospitality. I feel surrounded by an icy cold. My spontaneity has disappeared. At table I am sullen and silent; in my room I feel ill. At times, however, I am seized by an absurd joy. I dance, all alone, and hum – bizarre fits that I have rarely indulged in before now.

Since yesterday, my relations with Maitreyi and her family are back on their old footing of the most intense affection. As we were driving back from the office, I told Sen that Mantu had "misunderstood my view of marriage". I had said the right thing. Their coldness was due not to my avowed intention never to marry, as I had thought, but to quite another reason. Mantu had declared that I ridiculed marriage itself. The Indians do not know of a more sacred duty than the taking of a wife and the household could do nothing other than show me its heartfelt disapproval.

Maitreyi and I laughed a lot yesterday.

Today we talked for a long time in the library. We read "Shakuntala" together, seated on the carpet. Her private tutor arrived and I asked if I could sit through the lesson. In the evening, on the terrace, she recited some verses from Tagore's "Mahouya" by heart. After she had proclaimed them, magnificently, she became sombre and sad. Then she withdrew silently, without anyone noticing. Her last words of the day were poetry.

Do I love Maitreyi?

VII

Extracts from my diary of the following month:

We were alone, discussing manliness, Walt Whitman, Papini and the others. She has not read much but she listens. I know she likes me – she has told me so. She declared that she would give herself to a man – like Tagore's heroine – on the beach, at the start of a storm. Romantic nonsense?

My passion grows, a delicious mixture of romance, sensuality, companionship, devotion. When we are sitting next to each other on the rug, reading together, the slightest contact disturbs me. I feel that she too is troubled by it. Through literature, we communicate so much to each other. At times, we both sense that we desire each other.

A note added later:

Wrong. At that time, Maitreyi knew nothing of passion. She was taken up in the game, in the exquisite pleasure of a mock-sensuality, not in sensuality itself. She had no idea what passionate love meant.

Continuation of my diary:

First evening, first night in her room until eleven o'clock. We were translating Tagore's "Balaka" and talking... The engineer, back from a dinner in town, walked in on us. I, very calm, continued talking. Maitreyi lost her composure, snatched up the book and opened it. "We are studying Bengali," she said.

So, she knows how to lie?

Note added later:

No! How little I understood! She was not lying – she had

simply forgotten that I had stayed with her to translate "Balaka". When she saw her father, she remembered. If someone else had come in, she would have carried on with the conversation, but she could not speak in front of her father. So she went back to the book.

Continuation of my diary:

Today I brought her an enormous bunch of lotus. She took them into her arms and thanked me: her face disappeared behind the flowers. I am sure she loves me. She writes me poems and recites poetry to me all day long. I do not love her. I admire her. She disturbs me. Her body and her mind are overwhelming.

I have discovered a new trait in her personality. One evening, I was speaking to Lilu and threatened to repeat certain things she had just told me to Mantu.

Lilu simpered, "What could he do to me?"

"I've no idea," I replied "I have no experience of domestic quarrels."

"He will punish her, one way or another," Maitreyi declared, stressing the words "one way or another."

She repeated the expression, laughing, when we were alone. So she knows ...? She also told me that she wants to give herself, in a moment of madness, intoxicated with love or with lyricism. She tells me these things with an incredible candour. I would not have believed, at the beginning of our friendship, that she would ever confide in me in such a way.

Note added later:

In fact, Maitreyi was playing a game, nothing more. Lilu had explained marital love to her but she had understood nothing – she was merely repeating expressions which amused her.

Continuation of my journal:

Maitreyi, Lilu, Mantu and I went to a local cinema, to see an Indian film starring Himansural Ray. Maitreyi and I sat next to each other. We talked a lot. And how we laughed! But as we were leaving the auditorium, she had an hysterical fit and fainted. Why? The darkness, the subject of the film or an entirely physical upset brought about by our proximity? I know that she is incredibly sensual, whilst remaining quite pure. That is the miracle of the Indian woman. My Bengali friends have educated me on that: a young virgin becomes on her wedding night, it seems, a skilled and perfect lover.

Maitreyi has hinted at some romance with a beautiful young man, a Bengali studying in England. Does she really have to follow the idiotic itinerary of every mediocre sentimental attachment?"

Note added later:

She had simply wanted to banish from her mind experiences she had before she knew me and to let me know of her renunciation.

Continuation of my diary:

I brought her flowers again. She was angry because I also gave some to the others and to Mrs Sen. I think Mantu has noticed our intimacy: whenever we are alone, he interrupts us without ceremony and even if Maitreyi tells him we are having a "private talk", he insists on staying with us.

I went to the cinema with the engineer. He told me sadly that his trip to France had been postponed. Did I imagine it or did he hint at my eventual marriage to his daughter? Coming back in the car, I again asked myself if I loved Maitreyi. I know that the image of our nuptial bed obsesses and torments me.

I have taken to an amusing strategy. I avoid meeting her. I pretend I am frightened of her, am madly in love with her. She wanted to speak to me this morning and almost forced herself into my room. Such intimacy with a young Indian girl is unheard-of. How will it all end? I simply do not know. She disturbs, fascinates me – but I am not in love. I am amusing myself, nothing more.

Unexpected about-turn. I was wrong to go too far, to feign child-like devotion. I had thought it would be the surest route to an Indian girl's heart. Yet Maitreyi is more than just an Indian girl, she has a unique intelligence, served by an extra-ordinary will. She dislikes devotion. She cannot bear men to adore her: by telling me that, she was evidently including me among her admirers. She thinks the cult made of her banal and puerile. She hates and despises it. She dreams of an exceptional man who has gained supreme mastery over such sentimental idiocy. My attitude exasperates her...

Very well! If that is how it is, I shall change tactics. The sensual delight of our meetings evaporated with her admonition. So here I am in my new freedom, waiting in my room – with a lunatic impatience – for our next conversation. I want to see how she will react. I will show her I find her love laughable. I know she loves me and is attached to me. She cannot hide it. If we were alone together for twenty-four hours, she would give herself unhesitatingly.

But, my God, she insults me! Why does she tell me that ordinary love disgusts her? Does anything better exist?

No other woman has ever disturbed me in this way. My sensual suffering is torture in this scorching weather, when I have so much work. Is it the mystery of her body? I think so.

I am disturbed by conversations which hint at the great danger: my marriage to Maitreyi. Preparations are being made for that marriage – I am certain of it. New proof appears every day. Mrs Sen, in particular, cocoons me in maternal warmth. The engineer calls me "my child".

Last night, at dinner, Mrs Sen chided me for calling her "Mrs Sen", and not "Mama" in the Indian way. She is as sweet-natured as a saint and her sweetness is infectious. Her innocence calms and relaxes me. I love her.

I am bombarded by jokes and allusions. Mantu wants me to call him "Uncle" and Lilu "Aunt", even though she is only seventeen years old. It is all very amusing...

Upset with Maitreyi. We have quarrelled over nothing. This kind of conflict erupts between us at least twice a day.

She tried to pacify me by giving me all sorts of little caresses –
half sensual and half friendly. I shut myself up in my room and
worked, morosely. In fact, I had wanted to break our secret
and passionate friendship – although I was afraid I had gone
too far. I wanted to find some pretext on which to speak to her,
but it was unnecessary. It was she who apologized and our
game began again. I do not know if I can control myself for
much longer.

I almost kissed her today. We were alone in my room. It
demanded immense self-control to stop myself from taking
her in my arms. She was dangerously excited and I was beside
myself with desire. I managed to restrain myself to squeezing
her arm, biting it. I dared not go any further. I am frightened, I
have become an object of terror to myself.

Note added later:

I was mistaken, Maitreyi was not in the least excited. Simply,
she was troubled by my attitude. She was playing, nothing
more – it was I who pushed things to the limit...

Continuation of my diary:

Maitreyi is a girl such as one rarely encounters. As a wife,
would she not become as mediocre as any other woman?

Later in the evening she came back, dressed only in that
lovely crimson shawl which leaves her practically naked. It is
a Rajput costume, worn next to the skin, instead of over a tunic
in the usual Bengal fashion. Beneath the translucent material,
her brown breasts seemed slightly paler, a shade of damask, and
I was overwhelmed, terrifyingly, by that sight. I knew she had
put on that obscene and delicious costume for my benefit. The
engineer had gone out; she would not have dared wear it in his
presence.

She comes to my room continually, without pretext, and is
always provocative or malicious. She is magnificent in her
passion. Her body is indescribably seductive.

I force myself to think of her as ugly, too fat, reeking of
unsavoury scent. By means of this "meditation on created

images", I manage to control myself. But the truth is that my nervous system is tiring itself out, uselessly. I understand nothing any more. What are they hoping to achieve?

This morning, quarrel with Maitreyi. She took offence over some tiny fault I had committed and threatened not to speak to me for a week. I retorted that she could do what she wanted, it was of no importance to me. My words have heartened me. I am working better. Lilu came in the role of go-between to tell me that "the poetess is very upset". I replied that I was not angry, but if the game amused her she could go on with it...

So – how banal all women are, finally. In Europe, in Asia, intelligent or stupid, depraved or virgin, they all sing the same song...

This afternoon I went to the cinema, alone. I found it marvellously entertaining. At table, Maitreyi sat next to me, wearing a magnificent sari that was over a hundred years old. She was in tears. She said nothing and barely ate. "Mama" noticed at once and thanked me for talking to Maitreyi. After the meal, we had a little tête-à-tête. Maitreyi reproached me for having wrongly accused her, for having believed that she despised love, "friendship".

The battle lasted quarter of an hour. I took her hands, crushed them in mine. She was a charming sight, as she argued, grimaced, cried. She was doubtless invoking Tagore's help in her mind. She tried to free her wrists, which I held in a vice-like grip. We struggled. I remained calm, abandoning myself, without self-indulgence, detached and lucid, to the experience. She was finally forced to acknowledge my victory. Her joy at having been defeated was entirely sensual and mixed with bitterness: she was happy because I had mastered her but suffering because she had not received any help from her spiritual master, her guru.

I went with her to her room.

"You have covered me in bruises," she sighed, as we stood outside the door.

Without thinking, I took her hands, caressed them, kissed them. Such gestures are unthinkable in India. It would have been fatal for us to have been seen. A little later, without saying a word, she threw a flower into my room...

Cinema with Maitreyi and the others. She automatically took the seat next to mine. In the half-light, she whispered that we had important things to discuss. I replied, off-hand and non-chalant, that I found her "feelings" utterly laughable, that, in short, I detested her. She lost her regal calm and began to cry. I felt nothing.

Outside the cinema, she began sobbing once more. Involuntarily, I cried out "Maitreyi!" and then fell silent, over-come with embarrassment. That evening, she came into my room and cried again, her body shaken by nervous spasms, her face hidden beneath a shawl. She gave no explanation. She was, however, cool enough to burst into laughter a little later, when the others came to join her in my room.

Unexpected "reconciliation" with Maitreyi. She was stron-ger today, she cried only once and it was I who was nervous, helpless. I alluded to my imminent departure. The climax of the scene was played out against a backdrop of violence. I begged her to leave. I threw myself on the bed, hiding my confusion by feigning a fit. I was ridiculous. I promised her that our close "friendship" would revive. Faithful to my absurd strategy, I confessed dozens of lies which must have made me seem nauseatingly banal in her eyes. What a fool! She, on the contrary, kept splendidly calm. She acknowledged her own part in our sentimental "games". The knowledge that she has lowered herself in my eyes pains her. We must finish with all this, become just good friends again...

Entry made in my diary the following night:

Oh! It is not nearly so simple! I love her, I love her wildly and I am frightened of her. For her part, she suffers, she said, because of the pain she is inflicting on me.

I am afraid – and euphoric. My mind teems with new ideas,

new problems. For example: how can I love passionately without becoming sentimental? And yet! What does it matter whether or not I am becoming sentimental?

Am I drunk? Victim of my own practical joke? Today I was happy from dawn to dusk – filled, without logical reason, with an influx of energy, with a new appetite for the game.

I was on the point of asking Maitreyi: "Will you be my wife?" I am ready to propose to her, now, this moment. Married to her, I would be so happy, so purified, so at peace...

This afternoon, conversation with Maitreyi about marriage. I think about it all the time. I imagine myself married to her, head of a family, my life miraculously transformed into one of moral harmony. Contentment. Serenity.

In the evening, she tells me she is in despair: Tagore has not written to her. The poet is much more than a guru to her: he is a friend, a confidant, a fiancé, a god – perhaps a lover. She declares to me that "no one suspects their relationship". Love, Bengal-style. Am I jealous? Now that she knows everything, from my hints and confessions and from her own intuition, I decided to warn her that our love can never come to anything: "I cannot marry a woman who has loved another man before me," I told her.

She took my somewhat solemn and theatrical display of anger to heart. We did not meet after dinner: she sent a note through Khokha to say that I had offended her. I did not reply. This whole affair irritates and entertains me by turns. Mostly, it works on me like a poison. I dream of marriage, I picture my children, my sons. I waste my time. It is difficult to concentrate. But I cannot relinquish my passion.

Tonight, an earthquake. I am still feverish. I met Maitreyi this morning and gave her a very expensive book.

A day of extraordinary emotion, which is difficult to recount here. Briefly, Maitreyi picked a quarrel with me, asked me what my intentions in the relationship were. I continually betray myself and compromise her. Mantu and Khokha have already noticed many things... she cried, shaken by violent sobs. I did not say a word. I was sorry I had upset her, but I did not waver from my attitude of the greatest composure...

Unfortunately, at that moment Khokha happened to be on the veranda, passing my room. He must have heard everything. Maitreyi began crying even more bitterly, then with desperation. She wrote, on the back of an envelope, that she wanted to die. For an Indian girl, what Khokha had just overheard amounted to disgrace.

Eventually she calmed down. She tidied the table, rearranged the flowers. I said nothing.

Maitreyi has begun a book of poems entitled "Illusions and Beautiful Mirages".

Today, I told her of the freedoms that European girls enjoy. She asked me if I was pure; the mere thought that I might not be so appalled her that she began crying. The violence of that thirst for purity, almost mystical in its intensity, moved me.

In the evening, our conversation veered once more towards the subject of marriage. She told me that she will doubtless marry a young Bengali, who will make her unhappy. I confessed my principal sin to her: to ..ave been born white. Had I been born an Indian, I would have had far more chance of success with her. I am not sure how sincere I was being. She again became upset. I asked her the vital question: why were we forbidden to marry? Still as a statue, she looked at me and then all around, worried that I might have been overheard. She replied that fate, or indeed God, had ordained it thus. I asked her if it were not rather prejudice that was responsible. She answered that God manifested His will by such prejudices and that my love was perhaps nothing more than a temporary illusion...

In fact, this passion, which at first I had thought impossible, insignificant, sheer fantasy, which was inflamed by Maitreyi herself – who, I had so long believed, was in love with me but is, in reality, in love with no one – this passion has me in thrall and carries me far away, to an unknown and unearthly region of my soul, to some border territory of my mind where I am blissfully happy, radiant with grace. I have no name for that intimate realm.

I am thinking seriously about marriage.

Since that day, I have managed to see her only with great difficulty. She has stayed in her room, writing or singing. I sent her several innocuous notes through Lilu. She has not replied. The first night I imagined a whole host of things. A little less after. And then, nothing. Clearly, I can very easily live without Maitreyi.

VIII

One afternoon, several days later, I met Harold coming to ask me to a picnic. He seemed even colder and even nastier than usual.

"Is it true you are to marry the engineer's daughter?"

I reddened, and began joking, as I always do when I am embarrassed – especially if someone dear to me is involved. Harold ignored my quips and told me he had found out the news at work. He also knew that I was going to abandon my religion and take up Hinduism... He himself is nothing but a filthy sinner, who only sets foot in church to meet Iris, but he was visibly horrified by the idea of my conversion. He told me firmly that Narendra Sen was a monster, that I had been bewitched and that I would do well to give five rupees to the Little Sisters of the Poor to intercede for me.

I stopped him mid-flow.

"And the girls, how are they?"

"They miss you. You must be saving a lot, at Bhowanipore. You don't pay for your room or your board, you never go out to town. What do you do all day?"

"I'm learning Bengali for the Provincial Manager's exam," I lied, "and then it's a new world for me. I don't know how the time passes, but it does."

He borrowed five rupees to go to the YMCA ball that evening.

"You don't want to come?"

I did not. The memory of those profligate years at Wellesley Street and Ripon Street evoked neither sadness nor regret in me. I looked at Harold. This hulking fellow, with his swarthy face, magnificent eyes – a little shadowed – this companion of the night, with whom I had chased girls and wasted so much time, was now nothing more than a stranger to me. My new life seemed so pure, so sacred, that I dared not describe it to him. He promised to come and visit me soon and carefully noted down my address – doubtless, I thought, in anticipation of another, and larger, loan.

On my return, I found all Narendra Sen's family in the dining-room, having tea. Mantu and Lilu were there and Khokha with his two sisters – two of those shadow-women whom I almost never saw. I described my meeting with Harold to them frankly and confided my disgust at the life the Europeans and Anglo-Indians led in Calcutta – a life of which I had for so long been a part. My declaration delighted them. The women gazed at me intently and complimented me in their unintelligible jargon. Mantu shook my hand, closing his eyes as was his custom. Only the engineer did not congratulate me on that over-zealous condemnation of my race. He left us to read his inevitable detective story.

I went up on to the roof with Maitreyi, Khokha and Lilu. Stretched out on rugs, cushions under our heads, speaking little and shifting about to find the most comfortable position, we waited for night to fall. I had kept my sandals on. I moved my feet around, trying, by dint of casual, surreptitious movements, to lean them decently against the wall. Over the previous months, I had learnt a whole set of rituals: I knew, for example, that if I knocked into someone, I must bend down and touch his foot with my right hand, that I should never, even in jest, execute the gesture of a kick – and several other such precepts and prohibitions. I did not know what rites might surround the resting of feet against parapets. At that moment, I heard Lilu murmur something in Maitreyi's ear.

"She finds your foot very beautiful. It is as white as alabaster," Maitreyi explained to me, her expression filled with an unmistakable desire and sadness. I blushed, both from pleasure (believing myself ugly, any praise of my physical features delights me) and shyness. I did not know how to interpret Maitreyi's intense scrutiny of my legs. Her smile was one of contempt, wickedness, shame. To break the silence, I threw out some inept remarks and declared that the beauty of feet is irrelevant, since we never see them, at least in western cultures.

Maitreyi grew calmer.

"With us, it is different. Two friends show their affection for each other by rubbing their bare feet together. That is what I do whenever I talk with a friend. Look, like this...."

Quite flushed, she lifted the hem of her sari and went over to Lilu. Something curious then happened. Lilu began squeezing Maitreyi's leg between her ankles and Maitreyi quivered, smiling with pleasure as though she were being kissed. Those lazy sweeps along the calf, the clenched fingers, the heel pressed against the skin, followed by the kneading of flesh, warm and shuddering, against flesh, gave me the feeling I was watching the most intimate of love scenes. I was in agonies of jealousy and revulsion at that absurd contact between female bodies.

Abruptly, she took her leg away and pressed it against Khokha's large foot. I had to bite my lips, I could not bear it. I saw that black, dirty hoof, darkened by the sun and from walking on tar, come into sudden contact with Maitreyi's soft flesh – a contact warm with the promise of an entire body. Khokha smiled and quivered, as happy as a dog being stroked. To my regret, I could not see Maitreyi's eyes. I would have liked to read in them the sensuality that the trembling of that flesh, pressing against the flesh of the young man, betrayed. I remembered then the peals of laughter that Maitreyi would let loose at the witticisms of this ugly clown – they expressed the same abandon, the same desire to be possessed.

Later, I wondered if there were not ways of making love
other than those we know. Finer, less obvious ways: the secret
conquest of a woman by a caress or a witticism – or by intelligence, by which weapon she would belong to the beloved more
totally than in the most perfect, most ecstatic, of sexual unions.
For a long time after that evening, I was jealous, not only of the
poets and the musicians who gathered at Narendra Sen's – and
with whom Maitreyi chattered, smiled, laughed and discussed,
with obvious rapture, their art – but of every man who sent her
into fits of laughter. I was jealous of Khokha and of Mantu.
This last, more than all the others, tortured me: as her uncle, he
was permitted to squeeze her arm, to tap her on the shoulder, to
pull her hair. I found those innocent gestures more revolting
than any liberty a true rival might have taken. Maitreyi seemed
unconscious of the clandestine rape – both physical and mental
– perpetrated against her. But what tortured me most of all was
the spiritual rape. I was jealous of Acintya, a young poet – she
had met him only once but she spoke to him on the telephone
and sent him poems for the review *Prabudha Bharatta*. I was
jealous of a mathematician – he very rarely came to the house
but Maitreyi had spoken of him enthusiastically, declaring that
she liked great men. More than all the rest, I hated her guru,
Robi Thakkur... I tried, one day, to suggest to her, as delicately
as I could, that she gave herself too readily, intellectually as well
as physically. She had looked at me with an expression so
candid, so astonished, so honest, that I abandoned the
attempt...

The exchange of caresses between Maitreyi and Khokha left
me stunned, almost nauseous. I gritted my teeth and contemplated the first stars of the evening. The sky was still light. The
general conversation continued, in a colloquial Bengali that I
barely understood. I was not, in any case, trying to understand
it. The only sound I could concentrate on was Maitreyi's laugh.
Each time it rang out at Khokha's interminable puns or gri-
maces, a shudder went through me.

Maitreyi must have noticed my discomfort. She asked me, in English, if I were not too tired. Then, she asked if I would like to pass the time in my leisure hours by helping her finish the catalogue of her father's library. It would be a relaxation for me after my work at the office and we would have more opportunity to talk. It was true that over the last few days, I had hardly seen her.

It was the first I had heard of this catalogue. It seemed that Narendra Sen had acquired around 4,000 volumes, from legacies or purchases, and he wanted to have the collection listed in the form of a luxurious brochure so that he could more easily bequeath his books to a local college. I thought the project ridiculous, but I accepted.

"My father dared not ask you to help. He did not want you to give up too much of your time. I am just a girl, I have almost nothing to occupy me during the day and it will be an amusement for me to copy down the titles of books."

I remember that when I was alone that evening I cursed my foolishness. I had accepted the sacrifice of a large part of my free time far too readily. I knew the work would not be to my liking. And I was afraid that our game would start again, just as I had achieved some self-control.

The next day, before tea, Maitreyi was waiting for me at the entrance of the library.

"Come, I will show you what I have done."

She had placed several dozen books side by side on a table, spines uppermost, so that each title was visible.

"You start at this end of the table, I will start at the other. We will see which book we meet at."

She seemed to have been seized by some emotion. She looked at me, her lips trembling, blinking her eyelids as though forcing herself to forget something, to banish some image that had appeared before her.

I sat down to write, gripped by a curious premonition that another important incident was about to occur. Perhaps I hoped

that Maitreyi's love for me would be revealed. Perhaps some
spiritual communion, some insight into the depths of her darkness, was awaiting me. Suddenly, I realized that my sense of
expectancy was too mild. As I wrote, I wondered if I still loved
her. No. I was under the illusion that I loved her. Nothing more.
I realized yet again what it was in her that attracted me: the
absurdity, the unpredictability of her whole nature, her virginity – the virginity of a savage – and her power of seduction. I
was perfectly conscious of my state: I was bewitched, not in love.
It was curious that these revelations never came to me when I
was in my rational mind, but rather when I was on the brink of
some decisive experience, in the sudden illumination of those
moments when I felt I was living in reality, in all its fullness.
Cold reflection never revealed anything to me.

My hand fell on the next book and met Maitreyi's hand. I
started.

"What book have you got to?"

I showed her. It was the one that she, too, had reached: *Tales
of the Unexpected*, by Wells. All at once she blushed, with
pleasure or astonishment, I do not know.

"You see? Ah, what 'unexpected' is lying in wait for us?" she
said in a subdued voice. I smiled, also impressed by the coin-
cidence. In fact, most of the books on the table had portentous
titles: *The Dream, Take me with you!, Help me!, Nothing New*,
and so on. I was trying to think of a richly ambiguous reply
when Chabu called us for tea and we had to leave the room. We
were profoundly happy. We could not stop looking at each
other.

During tea, I expounded exuberantly on my recent reading
about Krishna and the vaishnav cult. I related episodes from
the life of Chaitanya with so much enthusiasm and sincerity
that Mrs Sen could not restrain herself. She came over to me,
profoundly moved.

"One would think you were a vaishnava yourself," she said,
two large tears in her eyes.

I was overjoyed by the compliment. I replied that I thought vishnuism one of the most sublime religions. Mantu and I began discussing belief while Maitreyi listened with distant eyes, silent. And then she suddenly burst out:

"You others, what do you know about religion?"

She blushed, then paled, became agitated, on the verge of tears. I sat stunned, wondering whether I should apologize for her outburst or try to explain it. Mantu went to comfort her but she tore herself away and ran to the library. I finished my tea, feeling helpless.

No one spoke. I retreated to my room to write letters, overcome with a disquiet and gnawing impatience that I had never known before. As I wrote, I suddenly felt I had to see Maitreyi. I went in search of her. That day was of great importance. An extract from my notes:

"I found her crushed, almost crying. I pretended I had come because she had called me. That declaration seemed to astound her. I left her for five minutes, to finish my letter. When I returned, she was asleep on the couch opposite the table. I roused her and she started. I studied her face. Her eyes seemed to have grown larger. She met my eyes steadily, asking repeatedly, her voice almost a whisper: 'What's the matter? What's the matter?'

"And then she became as incapable of speaking as I was. We gazed into each other's eyes, entranced, caught by the same preternaturally soft fluidity of that look, powerless to resist, to free ourselves from the dream. It is difficult to analyse my emotional state. It was a happiness at once calm and violent, to which my soul offered no opposition, a blossoming of the senses that took me beyond sensuality, that suffused me in an elysian bliss. It was a state of pure grace.

"At first, it was enough to look. And then our hands met. Savage embraces and sweetly devotional caresses followed – I have just read a book on love by Chaitanya and use, despite myself, this mystical language – which led, very naturally, to my kissing her hands. She was so lost in her ecstasy, she bit her lips with a passion so violent – and yet so pure! – that it would have been easy for me to risk everything and kiss her on the mouth. With immense effort, I controlled myself. The situation was dangerous. Anyone coming downstairs would see us. I asked her again why we were forbidden to marry. She trembled. In order to test her, I asked her to repeat the mantra Tagore had given her as a talisman against impurity. She obeyed, but the spell was not broken, proving what I already knew – our attraction was more than merely physical. It was love, love reflected by the body's sincerity. We had lived, confirmed, that miracle of human ascent into the supernatural through touch and sight. The experience lasted two hours and exhausted us. It will be renewed each time that our eyes meet."

Then she asked me to remove my sandals and to touch her foot with mine. I will never forget my emotion at that first contact: it was a happiness that compensated for all the jealousy I had suffered. I knew that in that sweet offering of her ankle, her leg, Maitreyi was giving herself to me completely – as she had never given herself to another. She could not have been deceiving me while touching me in that way. No lie could have been so divine. The episode on the roof had been eclipsed. Almost against my will, my foot climbed higher, towards the hollow behind her knee, towards that fold of flesh whose softness, and incredible warmth, I sensed. It was, without doubt, virgin territory. No man had ever dared explore so far.

During those two hours of kisses (were those mutual caresses of our ankles and our legs anything other than kisses?), I lived more intensely and I understood more profoundly Maitreyi's real being than during the previous six months, wasted in efforts of friendship and attempts at love. I had never been so sure, with an absolute certainty, that I possessed something.

I had still not told her outright that I loved her. I think we both knew it, instinctively. For a long time afterwards, I would believe that her every gesture held a message of friendship and affection. I had not the least doubt that she loved me or that she was equally certain of my love for her. So it was with sadness, bewilderment, that I saw her pull away from me, become speechless with terror, her eyes panic-stricken, or bury her face in her hands, each time that I spoke of our marriage. I did not understand her. Had not both she and her parents showered approval on my marriage plans?

I told her that I loved her. I was unable to see the effect my words had on her: she hid her eyes and said nothing. I moved closer to her and repeated, with greater warmth and sincerity, the few words of love that I could express in Bengali. She moved away.

"Leave me," she said, in a distant, cold voice. "I see you have not understood my love. I love you as a friend, as a very dear friend. I cannot love you differently, and I do not want to..."

"But we are not friends, we are in love!"

All at once, I had recovered my presence of mind and my clarity of thought.

"The soul knows many ways to love."

"Yes, but you are in love with me, it is useless to lie to yourself. We cannot live without each other, we have tortured ourselves enough by hiding the truth from each other. I love you, Maitreyi, I love you..."

I spoke in a torrent of confused words, mixing one Bengali word with five of English.

"Say that again, in your own language."

A stream of French – whatever came into my head – came pouring out. It was dark and all the lamps had been lit outside. I went to light the library.

"No, leave it," she said.

"What if someone comes? If we are found together in the dark?"

"What does it matter? In this house we are brother and sister."

I pretended not to understand. I went to her again and took her hands to kiss them.

"Why do you not want to understand certain things?"

Her voice was edged with laughter.

"Because those things are idiotic," I replied, very sure of myself and of her love.

Then unfolded an unexpected scene. Maitreyi began crying and released herself from my hands. She tried to leave the room. I imprisoned her in my arms and put my head in her hair, murmuring words of tenderness, trying to win her over. I begged her not to cry any more, to forgive me. But I could not resist the perfume, the warmth, the temptation of that sweet body – and I kissed her. She struggled and cried out, putting her hand against her mouth. I was frightened – we might be heard – and I let her go. She tore free, heaving a sigh that humiliated me. But instead of leaving, she moved over to the window. The light of the street lamp fell on to her and I trembled at the sight of those strange, desperate eyes, bathed in tears, and the dishevelled hair, spread across her shoulders. She bit her lips. She looked at me as though I were a ghost or a madman and pointed to where I had just kissed her. She could neither speak nor defend herself. I went to her and took her in my arms, covering her with fresh kisses, incapable in my madness of rational thought or action, as though drugged by my passion. I kissed her mouth and found warm, tender, perfumed lips – lips such as I would never have believed I would one day kiss. At first, they tightened defensively beneath mine but when she had almost no more strength left, I felt them relax, become willing to be kissed, bitten... I could feel her breasts against me. Her body gave itself to mine – with such abandon that I felt a touch of melancholy that she should give herself so readily.

I do not know how long that first embrace lasted. Suddenly, she began struggling, as though she were suffocating. I let her go. She fell in a heap at my feet. I thought she had fainted and I bent down to help her, but she grasped my legs and, sobbing, begged me not to touch her any more. She beseeched me, in the name of God, the name of my mother, the name of Mrs Sen... I shuddered and did not speak. I let her get up. She dried her tears abruptly, arranged her hair, looked at me long and searchingly and then left, heaving a great sigh.

I went back to my room in a state of extreme agitation, filled with a torrent of emotions – joy at having won her, pride, then remorse, and fear for the future. I could do nothing before dinner. I wondered if I would have the courage to speak to her at the table. Above all, I wondered what she must think of me. I was frightened that she might confide in her mother or Lilu – I was certain of nothing, believed in nothing, any more.

She did not come down to the meal. However, as soon as it was over, Lilu came to me.

"The poetess sends you this letter."

With bated breath, I opened the message. It was written in French so that no one else would understand: "Come morning six o'clock library."

IX

I did not leave for work until ten, but the morning tea was served at eight. We therefore had two hours to speak together in peace. I had slept badly, plagued by fever and nightmares. I dreamed that I had lost Maitreyi, that an angel with a white beard was chasing me from the house while Narendra Sen looked on, with a distracted air, from the roof. I woke again and again, trembling, my forehead icy cold and damp. I felt heavy with guilt, as though I had committed a mortal sin.

Maitreyi was in the library, dressed in a white sari, a grey shawl thrown over her shoulders. She was filling in cards for the catalogue. I greeted her, horribly embarrassed: I did not know whether I should kiss her, smile at her or behave as if nothing had happened. I am always at a loss when I meet a lover after a decisive incident has occurred; I need all my powers of concentration and imagination to handle the situation and I have to know what is expected of me. My every gesture poses a problem. I contradict myself. I apologize. I am ridiculous.

Maitreyi seemed calm and resolute – although the shadows around her eyes and the pallor of her face were testimony to a night spent in prayer and meditation. (Was I mistaken? I was sure that I had heard, towards morning, her voice repeating a monotone chant. The prayer stopped and started, stopped and started – and then suddenly there was no more, as if it had been broken off by a sob). I sat down opposite her on a seat she had made ready for me. I began to write, mechanically, copying book titles on to cards. I kept my eyes focused on the work.

"Did you sleep well?" I asked her after several minutes, to break the silence.

"I did not sleep at all," she replied calmly. "I think it is time that you left our house. That is why I called you here..."

I tried to interrupt, but she made a desperate, imploring gesture and I fell silent, feeling more and more ill at ease. As she spoke, she scribbled in pencil on a sheet of paper, without looking at me. She drew, then erased, she wrote phrases that I could not make out, added signs and figures that I could not understand. This game reminded me of the early days of our friendship and of our first French lessons. I almost upbraided her for the mistakes in the note she had sent me the night before, but I realized that the moment was hardly appropriate for such a jest and said nothing.

Maitreyi left me little time to dwell on my thoughts. She began telling me things I could barely believe, that disturbed me, shocked me, wounded my pride and overturned all my convictions. She had never spoken for so long without changing the subject, without stopping to question me, or waiting for me to reply or to comment. She spoke as though she were alone in the room and I no longer existed for her.

I had been wrong to believe that she loved me in the way that I loved her. Her heart had long since belonged to another, to Robi Thakkur. She had loved him since she was thirteen, since she had read his books. She had spent every summer except the last at Shantiniketan, staying with the poet's family, in his own house. How often, at night, alone with the old man on the terrace and seated at his feet, had she listened to him talking! He had stroked her hair. At first, she had not known what emotion it was that transported her beyond ordinary consciousness into a never-ending, unspeakably exquisite dream. She had thought that the veneration and filial devotion she had for her guru must have caused the miracle. Then, one evening, the poet had told her that it was in fact a manifestation of Love. She had fainted. She did not know how long it had been before she came round, laid out in the poet's room, on his bed, her face covered in perspiration. The fresh smell of jasmine floated through the room. Her guru was still stroking her hair. It was then that he had given her the mantra that protected against impurity. He had asked her to stay pure for the rest of her life, to write poetry, to love, to be faithful to him and never to forget him. And she never had forgotten him. She kept the letters he had written her, from every corner of the world, in a box made of perfumed wood which he had given her two years ago, with a lock of his hair...

Disgusting old charlatan! Corrupter of young girls! I raged to myself, burning with jealousy, fury, impotent outrage, with his libidinous mysticism, his vile mixture of devotion and trickery! How could I have believed in her purity? How could I have believed that I was the first man to have touched her?

Apparently, however, her guru had never kissed her. He had simply stroked her hair. And she had not seen him for a long time. He was always abroad, travelling. And then, and then – oh, that slight hesitation! – Mrs Sen had, it seemed, observed certain emotional excesses in her daughter's behaviour. Maitreyi was no longer allowed to see her guru. But she had not forgotten him for a moment. She wanted us to be good friends. I could share in that mystical tenderness, we would love him together... I had never been anything other to her than a friend. The possibility that she could love me in any other way had never occurred to her. Our game should have stayed a game, we should never have touched or kissed. As she spoke these last words she blushed, becoming almost inaudible and making great mistakes in her English. Then she continued in Bengali. She had always had a sincere and warm affection for me. As a friend, she liked me very much, she enjoyed being with me, she was happy when we joked together, when we gazed at each other, when we held hands – but all that was nothing more than simple friendship. If I had thought it was something else, that was her fault: she had hidden too many

things from me, she had led me to believe complete fantasies –
that she was in love with me, for instance...

When, pale and visibly tired, she had finished, I stood up,
only half conscious, numb, blank. I went towards her. Maitreyi
looked at me with a fear that was tinged with compassion. I took
her head in my hands and, knowing she could neither cry out
nor call for help, kissed her on the lips. We were both conscious
that someone might come down the upper staircase at any
moment and see us. But the risk somehow only incited me to
prolong the kiss, until she was almost suffocating. I relaxed my
grasp.

"Why do you do that? I am weak. You know I cannot resist. I
feel nothing when you kiss me. It is as if your lips were those of
Chabu, of a child. They do not affect me. I do not love you..."

I left for work immediately, without having tea. Maitreyi's
declarations had reassured me in some way, despite my fury
and my jealousy. The girl seemed incapable of doing anything
that went against her innermost nature.

When I returned in the evening I did not look for her and did
not meet her. At dinner, she took her usual place on my right.
Only Mantu, Lilu, Maitreyi and I were there. The talk was of
politics: the arrest of the mayor, Sarojini Naidu's speech, the
vast numbers of people who had been imprisoned during the
civil war. I vowed to myself that I would not look at Maitreyi, or
touch her, even by accident. Suddenly, however, I felt her
warm and naked foot being placed tremblingly on mine. The
shudder that ran through me must have betrayed my feelings.
She lifted the hem of her sari, without anyone noticing, and my
leg stroked hers. I no longer tried to resist the bewitching
pleasure, the warm sensuality that suffused me. Her face was
ashen, her lips full red and she looked at me with penetrating,
terror-stricken eyes, while her body called out to me, inviting
me; I had to dig my nails into my chest to bring myself back to
sanity. Our disturbed state can hardly have escaped the others'
notice.

After that, the embrace of our legs and our knees beneath the table became a daily pleasure; it was the only time that I could caress her in that way. If I had touched her with my hand, she would have considered it an act of disgusting lechery and would immediately have doubted the purity of my feelings.

As we were leaving the dining-room, she stopped me.

"Would you like to see how much I have done?"

She lit the lamp in the library, but then, instead of going over to the table where all the cards were laid out, went into the other room, which had no lamp. She looked all around to make sure that no one could see us and then held out her arm, naked to the shoulder.

"Try anything you want, kiss it, caress it, you will see that I feel nothing..."

Long before, we had discussed eroticism. I had declared that someone who truly knew how to love could experience full sensual pleasure on the tiniest contact with the body of the beloved. I had added that, for me, sexual possession is far more mysterious and complicated than we imagine. It is almost impossible to truly have something, to obtain it, conquer it. Rather than possessing, we only believe we possess.

I had thrown out these clichés casually, convinced that Maitreyi would not be able to grasp anything more subtle or profound. Yet my words had tormented her to such an extent that she was now using this "essence of eroticism", of which I had spoken, to test her own feelings. I took her arm and looked at it for a moment, fascinated. It was no longer the arm of a woman. It now had such a transparency, a warmth, that it was as though Passion itself – in all its desire to conquer – had been condensed into that matt brown skin. It had taken on a life of its own; it no longer belonged to the young girl who held it out to me, as though in front of fire, to test her own love. I took it between my hands like a live offering, disturbed by its trembling and by the strangeness of what I was about to do. I began caressing it, stroking it, bathing it in kisses – and as I did so, I was certain that I was kissing Maitreyi's entire body. I felt her crumpling beneath the passion, giving into it as though she were in agony. Then, like someone waking at first light, she came to life. As I kissed her, I saw her face blanch. Her eyes were blazing. Her willpower was weakening: the appeal that I was making, on the naked flesh of her arm, spoke to her entire being and the light touch of my fingers, as they moved towards her shoulder, spread throughout her body.

She seemed about to fall: she leaned on me more and more heavily, and then put her free arm around my shoulder and clutched me, crying and catching her breath. After a few moments, her body relaxed, as though she were offering herself freely to me. I kissed her on the mouth. It was no longer a kiss of violation: her lips opened voluntarily, her teeth bit me gently and the rigidity of her body was not now resistance or even a passive offering of herself, but a tension strung to my desire. I knew then that all her confusion and her troubled thoughts about another man had faded, like shadows dissolving at the approach of daybreak: the daybreak of her sexuality. An unknown beatitude flooded every particle of my being and enraptured my body; in that plenitude, I recognized my truest self. A wave of joy lifted me out of myself, without dividing or destroying me, or pushing me towards madness. Never had I lived so immediately in the present as I did during those few minutes, when I seemed to live outside of all time. That embrace was something much more than love.

She came to herself, covered her eyes with her hands, the palms outermost, and moved away from me, the spell broken. She threw little glances at me, trembling and hiding her face. Then, abruptly, she went over to the table and said in an expressionless voice, showing me the books:

"This is what I have done today."

A supernatural foresight had inspired her words. At that moment, Khokha appeared and announced that Mrs Sen was

calling her from her room upstairs. I put out the lamps, trying
to compose myself. I was so excited, my senses so drunk, that I
almost confided my violent, undeserved happiness to Khokha.

Back in my room, I could not keep still. I stared out of the
barred window, threw myself on the bed, got up and paced the
floor. I wanted to see Maitreyi again, to go to sleep with the
picture of her face imprinted in my mind, with the memory of
her lips on mine – to see her without threat of the arrival of
some Khokha... We had not left each other as we should have
done. The intimacy we had shared demanded an embrace, a
farewell kiss. I was certain that Maitreyi felt the same: I could
hear her walking in her room with a soft tread, go out on to the
balcony, come back in... Whenever she approached the window, her shadow was thrown on to the wall opposite. Her light
went out and I stood there motionless, filled with a curious
sense of regret.

Then I heard whistling. It sounded like a tune, but I knew its
real meaning. I went over to the window and gave an answering
whistle. No reply. I thought she was on the balcony. With great
caution, I opened the room of my door and then the heavier one
of the corridor and went out on to the veranda. I dared not go
down to the street: the beam of light from the lamp was too
bright.

I whistled again.

"Alain! Alain!"

It was the first time she had used my name. I looked out and
caught sight of her, leaning against the balustrade, wearing only
a shawl that she had thrown over her shoulders. Her black hair
flowed over the length of her arm and that almost naked figure,
standing under the soft, filtered light, framed by sprigs of
wisteria, looked like the illustration to some Oriental tale.

I contemplated her in silence. The soft fluidity of her arms,
the head leaned against her shoulder in a gesture of resignation,
showed that she, no more than I, had not the strength to speak.
We looked at each other. And then she slid her fingers under-

neath her shawl, took something white from between her
breasts and threw it down to me. I watched its slow descent.
It was a little wreath of jasmine. A second later, before I could
speak, she had disappeared. Contented and appeased, I went
back to my room, closing the doors as carefully as before.

I met Khokha in the corridor.   .

"I am getting some fresh water," he said uneasily, before I
had even spoken. It did not occur to me, then, that the reason
he was continually loitering might be that he was spying on us.

I clutched the little wreath of jasmine, filled with too much
solace and joy to think of anything else. Later, I found out that
it was a symbol of engagement: a girl who offers such a wreath
to a young man is considered to belong to him forever – no
circumstance, not even death, can break the link between them.
But I did not know that then. It was because the flower came
from Maitreyi, had lain against her bosom, that I squeezed it
between my fingers, that I thought it a treasure beyond price.
Its perfume evoked the seductiveness of Maitreyi's lips. I sat on
my bed, gazing at it, and all at once my thoughts went back to
the moment of our first meeting. I remembered that I had
found Maitreyi ugly. I would never have dreamed then that
we would one day be joined in intimacy – and yet I knew,
despite my refusal to acknowledge it, that I had loved her from
that moment.

The night passed in a continual see-saw of dream and memory. For the first time, I thought I heard the flamingos of Bengal
crying out above the flooded plains at the edge of the gulf. I saw
the world open behind an archway of joy and a noble, mythic
existence hold out its promise in the sky, above an earth overrun with snakes, that echoed to the sound of village drums and
on which we walked, Maitreyi and I, through fields and mountains, like the very first lovers.

The following day, a heavy load of work kept me at the office
and I did not come back until long after dinner was over.
Maitreyi was waiting for me in the dining-room. She had

brought the cards with her and was filing them alphabetically in a box. She paled when she saw me and immediately busied herself with laying out my meal. Then she came to sit next to me, her shawl drawn down low across her forehead, and studied my face. I was painfully unsure of what to say, frightened of appearing vulgar. I was tired and I ate eagerly. I wanted to appease my hunger while showing her by my expression that I had not forgotten her, that she was still as precious to me as she had been the night before.

"Did you think of me today?"

I knew that lovers asked each other such questions. But it seemed to have real meaning for her: she had closed her eyes and I saw two tears, or rather two shining dots which lay, suspended, at the edge of her eyelids.

"Why are you crying?"

I was conscious that I wanted to appear more troubled than I really was. And yet, my God, I loved her! I loved her like a madman! Why then was I unable to share her suffering? How could I think of my hunger when she was crying?

She said nothing. I got up from the table and stroked her hair. Then I went back to my meal.

"Alain, I want to show you something." She spoke in Bengali, so as to use the familiar 'you' form to me (the monotony of English sentences exasperated her: she found the constant use of the second person plural abhorrent), her voice taking on the most melodious and feminine of inflections.

She showed me the box that Tagore had given her. It contained a curl of perfumed white hair.

"Do what you like with it. Burn it if you want. I cannot keep it any more. I did not love Tagore, my passion for him was a madness. He should have been nothing more to me than a guru. I thought I loved him in another way – but now I know..."

She looked as me as though she were dreaming. That look penetrated me, enveloped me as if to transform me into some creature that her desire had conjured up, a creature who was

perhaps still Alain, but an Alain who was brighter, warmer, less
flawed.

"Today I love only you. I have never loved before. I thought
that I loved. Now I know. It is something different." She
wanted me to kiss her but I caught sight of Mantu and contented myself with squeezing her arm. I gave the box back to
her. It would have been ridiculous to wreak vengeance on a
wretched lock of white hair. And what did her past, her memories, have to do with me? I was so convinced that I was her first
and her only lover that her past held no terror for me. It did not
torture me then – as it would later, each time I felt her slip away
from me, to compare me, perhaps, with the other, or to dream
of a time before I had appeared in her life: a time that would
torment me because of its impenetrable mystery.

She misinterpreted my gesture, took it for a rejection, for
indifference towards her sacrifice.

"You do not want to take the hair?" she asked, shocked and
incredulous.

"What would I do with it? Burn it yourself, that would be
better."

"But it no longer has any value for me!"

Bemused, I took the box and placed it carefully in the inside
pocket of my jacket. Then I went to bathe. I whistled so good-
humouredly as I splashed myself with cold water that Lilu, who
was passing through the courtyard, came and asked me
through the steel walls of the hut if I had had a bad dream.
That seemingly nonsensical remark had its explanation in my
sadness of the previous month. I had tried to explain the deep
despondency into which the "Maitreyi problem" – as I called it
in my diary – plunged me by saying that I was having nightmares. The memory of that time of uncertainty and suffering
made my new joy and confidence seem all the more powerful. I
went back to my room, my body suffused with a warm sensuality, my mind with a sense of triumph.

I was finishing dressing when Maitreyi knocked on my door.

She came in and pulled the curtain across the doorway. It would have been too risky to close the door. She threw herself into my arms.

"I can never live without you..." she said softly. I kissed her. She struggled and made as if to leave.

"Is this not a sin?"

"But why?" I reassured her, "We love each other."

"We love each other without Mama's knowledge, or Papa's..." she replied, her whole body shaking with emotion.

"We will tell them soon."

She looked at me as if my words were the ravings of a lunatic.

"It is impossible to tell them such a thing!"

"Even so, we must. Soon. I have to ask for your hand. I will tell them we love each other: your father will not be able to refuse. You know how much he cares for me. He brought me to live here, he encouraged me to become your friend..."

I could not go on. Maitreyi's face expressed a deep, extraordinary suffering. I went to her, tried to take her in my arms, but she tore herself fiercely from my grasp.

"There is something you do not know. You do not know that we love you," she hesitated and continued, "that they love you, the family, in a very different way. I am also supposed to love you in that way and not as I do. I am supposed to love you like at the beginning, like a brother..."

"Don't talk nonsense!" I exclaimed, kissing her arm. "Me, your brother? Even your parents cannot think I should be that."

"Yes, yes. You do not know."

She began crying.

"O Lord, O Lord, why all this?"

"Do you regret it?"

She pressed against me.

"You know that I don't. Whatever happens, I will love only you. I am yours. One day you will take me back to your country, won't you? I will forget India. I want to forget it..."

She caressed me, in tears, enveloping my body in a great surge of sweetness, with an assurance that I would scarcely have expected in a girl who had kissed someone on the lips for the first time the day before.

"Say nothing to them. They will never accept that I marry you. They like you because they want you to become one of them, to become their son."

That information both astonished and delighted me. But she added, trembling:

"They said to me 'Maitreyi, from now on you will have a brother, Alain. You must love him as a brother. Father wants to adopt him. When Father retires, we will all go back to Alain's country with him. With our money, we will be able to live like rajahs. In his country, it is not hot, there are no revolutions, and the whites are not evil like the English are here.' And what have I done? Instead of obeying them, you see in what way I love you! You see in what way!"

I had to take her in my arms: she was about to fall. I sat her in the armchair. I felt dazed. We stayed there for a long time, not speaking a word.

X

A new kind of life began. I could fill a notebook on each of those days; so rich were they, so freshly have they stayed in my memory. It was the beginning of August, the holiday period. We spent nearly all our time together. I went back to my room only to change, to write up my journal and to sleep. Maitreyi was preparing for her Bachelor of Arts by private lessons and I was helping her. Together, we would listen to the pandit's commentary on "Shakuntala" for hours at a stretch, seated next to each other on a rug. I did not understand a word of the Sanskrit text, but I could squeeze Maitreyi's hand in secret, kiss her hair, tease her. During all this, the pandit – a very short-sighted man – corrected her translation or her replies to the grammar questions he put to her.

She explained the "Kalidasa" to me. She was expert at finding in every one of its verses on love a detail that corresponded to our own secret passion. My devotion to her was now such that I could love only what she loved – in music, literature, Bengali poetry. I tried to unravel several vaishnava poems in the original, I read and was deeply moved by the translation of "Shakuntala". I had discarded all that had previously captivated me; I was able to contemplate my volumes of physics – so carefully collected – without regret. I had renounced everything but my work and Maitreyi.

Several days after her last revelation, she came to tell me that she had hidden something else from me. I was so certain of her love for me and the taste of that sensual desire which her presence always aroused in me was so strong that I could not stop myself from taking her into my arms and covering her with kisses.

"No, you must listen. You must know everything. Have you ever loved anyone as you love me?"

"Never."

I replied without thinking, not knowing whether it was a lie or simple exaggeration. In any case, how could those ephemeral, physical affairs of my adolescence compare to this passion, which obliterated everything else and which had refashioned my soul into the soul and the will of Maitreyi?

"Neither have I. But I have had other lovers. Can I tell you about them?"

"If you want."

"First of all, I loved a tree, a 'seven leaves' as we call them here."

I burst out laughing and caressed her with a rather ridiculous gesture of protectiveness and benevolence.

"That is not love, my dear child!"

"Yes, it is. It is love. Chabu also loves her tree. Mine was bigger. We lived at Alipur then. There were many huge trees there. I fell in love with a 'seven leaves' that was enormous, magnificent – yet it was so kind, so soft to touch. I could not leave him. We kissed each other all day, I spoke to it, I kissed it, I cried. I composed poetry in my head and recited it to no one but him. Who else would have understood me? And when he caressed me by brushing his leaves against my forehead, I felt such a tender happiness that I could not breathe. I had to lean against the trunk, so as not to fall. At night, I would leave my room, all naked, and climb into my tree. I could not sleep alone. I cried and shivered up there in the branches until sunrise. Once Mama almost caught me. I was so terrified that I was ill and had to stay in bed for several days. That was the beginning of my heartache. I could stay in my bed only if they brought me, every morning, some freshly cut branches from my 'seven leaves'..."

I listened to her as though she were reciting a story. I could feel her distance from me. How complicated her soul was! Once more I saw that it was civilized people who were simple, innocent and clear. These Indians, whom I loved so much that I wanted to become one of them, all nurtured in the recesses of their beings a whole impenetrable history and mythology. How deep, complex and unintelligible they seemed to me!

Maitreyi's disclosure pained me. She seemed capable of loving everything with an equal fervour and I wanted, desperately, that she love no other but me! What greater torture can a lover undergo?

I visualized her, a naked child hugging a tree with fierce passion. The image disturbed and frustrated me. I would never be able to give her the pleasure she had experienced in that embrace – nor could I efface its memory from her mind. What else had it been, that union with leaves and branches, but love? Several questions plagued me afterwards. How had she given herself? How had those seven-fingered leaves made her naked flesh quiver with delight? What words had she uttered when she had felt herself possessed for the first time by her tree, and had submitted herself, body and soul, to him?

She had brought me, rolled in silver paper, a sprig of pressed leaves, dried and perfumed. Seized by a rush of uncontrollable fury, I snatched up the branch, looked at it with contempt and then, unable to restrain myself, reduced it to dust between my fingers.

"He wanted to do that too, but I stopped him."

I paled. So he had loved her as passionately as I, had suffered the same agony at knowing himself preceded in love by a tree! Where had all my fine confidence gone, my certainty that I was her first love? Maitreyi began kissing my hands. She assured me she had forgotten everything, her tree and her guru, that she loved me alone and that her other loves had been different 'from now'. I was silent. A sharp pain was coursing through me.

Then, something unleashed itself in me and I flinched before
an involuntary inner fury, the like of which I had never known.

"If you had not been my only lover, I would not have had the
courage to confess all that," she said, in tears. "You must tell
me about the girls you loved before me."

"I have never loved before."

She said, incredulously:

"How could you have lived without love? You are older than
me. How many times you must have been caught by love..."

I hesitated, reflecting. Maitreyi divined my thoughts. "No,
not your affairs, not the girls you seduced. I do not want to
know about them. That was dirt, not love..."

She began sobbing. At that moment, the chauffeur passed
the room. He stopped, astonished by the sound, and then
scuttled off furtively. Later, I found out that he, too, was
spying on us.

Maitreyi tried to control herself and covered her mouth with
the edge of her shawl. Suddenly, she cried out:

"Why do you torture me? Why do you think that my love
and my body are not pure?"

I stood rooted to the spot. I, torture her? Her revelations tear
me to shreds and it is she who protests? I said nothing. I loved
her like a madman, I could not withstand my passion or hers. I
wished with all my being that her past could disappear, but it
was she who continually paraded it before me, she who continually relived it in my presence.

She also told me, that afternoon, of another childhood love.
She had been twelve or thirteen. Her mother had taken her to
the large Jaganath temple at Puri. Caught up in the procession,
they were walking the length of the gloomy passageways that
surround the sanctuary when someone had approached
Maitreyi and, without her noticing, placed a garland of flowers
around her neck. When they emerged into the light, Mrs Sen
saw the garland, asked her daughter how she had got it and took
it from her, placing it around her own arm. However, as soon as

they had re-entered the darkness, Maitreyi felt another garland being slipped around her. Mrs Sen again removed it and took hold of her daughter's arm. But each time they entered a tunnel another garland was put around Maitreyi's neck; at the end of the procession, Mrs Sen was carrying six of them. She looked around angrily for the culprit: such a garland placed around a girl's neck is a symbol of engagement. And then a young man had appeared. He was extraordinarily beautiful, with a long mane of black hair flowing over his shoulders, penetrating eyes, bright red lips (how her description of that handsome stranger pained me); he had prostrated himself before Mrs Sen, touched her foot, said "Mama!" and then disappeared back into the crowd.

She had loved that young man for years, even after she had begun to love Tagore. (I held on to that detail: perhaps Maitreyi had also continued loving her guru after she had started to love me... and might not another man come, later, whom she would love at the same time as me?) She had told the poet about the incident. He had said that the young man was a messenger of Love and that those garlands possessed some symbolic meaning...

Listening to all this, I was horrified at the jungle that lay hidden in Maitreyi's mind and soul. What dark depths, what tropical flora of symbols and signs, what humid droplets of eroticism and expectation! Where was I in all that? I loved a young virgin of sixteen who had never before been kissed on the lips.

"Now I am yours, yours alone," Maitreyi declared, encircling me with her arms. "You taught me what love is. You made me tremble with pleasure. I have given myself to you. When you crumbled the leaves in your hand, I was happy. It makes me happy to see you as furious as a tempest. I want you to throw me to the floor, to treat me as nothing... That is how much I love you. So why are you frightened?"

It was true that I had no reason to be worried. Maitreyi

continually came to my room after the evening meal, when all
the others were asleep upstairs underneath the fan. She would
sit in the huge bamboo chair and virtually offer herself to me.
My kisses now covered her entire body, gliding down the
length of her neck to her bare shoulders, beneath her shawl
to her arms, her breasts. The first time I kissed her breasts, a
shudder went through her whole body and she went stiff.
Then, relaxing, she opened her bodice, her eyes filled with a
mixture of terror and pleasure. As though mad, driven, she
offered her breasts to me, doubtless awaiting the thunderbolt
that would annihilate us both. Her breasts were more lovely
than those carved by any sculptor and the dark pallor of that
body, laid bare of its covering for the first time, inflamed me.
Maitreyi was desire incarnate, her face immobile, her eyes fixed
on me as though I were the embodiment of some god.

There was more than sensuality in that shudder that ran
through her and left her corpse-like at my side. While I
retained my lucidity, handling my experience of love with
rationality, she gave herself up to it as though it had a divine
origin, as though the first contact of her virginal body with that
of a man were some supernatural event. Later I was to understand how much that first profound response of her body had
tortured her. With one hand she grasped the back of the chair,
with the other she caressed my hair. With immense effort, she
asked me:

"Is this not a sin?"

I replied, as I always did, with some inane reassurance, and
continued my caresses. Every so often I looked at her; such
complete abandonment astonished me: her head tilted back
and her eyes closed, she was crying. Her tears slid the length
of her cheeks, adhering stray locks of hair to the corner of her
mouth, her chin.

"When we are married, we will love each other without
limits," I said to her, to comfort her. "I will possess you completely."

"But now, is it not a sin?"

"Now I am only kissing you, caressing part of your body. Later it will be different, you will be mine, mine..."

"Am I not yours now? Is it not a sin?"

She closed her eyes as she said this, screwing up her eyelids and biting her lips.

It was several days before I understood what she meant. She believed she was committing a sin because her body responded with such ecstasy, that by wasting such a precious gift, she was disturbing the harmony of the universe. The moment she had given me her lips and had kissed me, pressing her body against mine, we had been united and if that union were not now taken to its conclusion, sensuality would turn to corruption and the joy of our love to carnal misery. The sin was not in allowing our bodies to explore more and more of each other but in putting a limit on our physical love. She was experiencing ultimate pleasure without allowing the fruit of that pleasure to be born and to grow. In the eyes of an Indian woman, such a waste was sinful. We should follow the law of tradition, marry, and from our embraces would be born the seeds of life, children... If we did not, our love would wither, our joy would become sterile and our liaison corrupt.

I realized, not without bitterness, that it was not eroticism or love that prompted her to ask me such a thing but rather superstition, a fear of karma, of gods, of ancestors. That night, I wondered where an honest expression of the senses, a real innocence of the body, were to be found – in Indians or in us, the civilized? Had not Maitreyi acted like one entranced, an automaton, since the day of our first kiss? Were not her 'spontaneous' surges of passion, and the grandeur of her love, simply the prosaic, inevitable consequences of her initial surrender, the fulfilment of the rites demanded by her primitive and superstitious conscience? I began to cut short our meetings, to avoid those prolonged embraces as much as I could. I was very fond of Mrs Sen and I respected her husband.

I wanted to ask for Maitreyi's hand in marriage and I resolved that I would do so as soon as a favourable occasion presented itself.

Until then, I preferred the warmer, more restrained communion that we shared in our excursions, by car, into the surroundings of Calcutta. We would wander – often until midnight – around Barackpur, Hooghly, Chandernagor. We were always accompanied by several members of the family but for us it was as if only we two were present – we were oblivious to any outside presence. Nothing intruded on our intimacy. How many villages we visited together! How many houses beneath palm-trees, hiding places that we fondly imagined as our own, we glimpsed in the distance! How many memories we sowed on those roads, plunged into shade by the seemingly unending columns of trees! By how many lakes we sat, furtively holding hands while the others went to fetch the baskets of food from the car! How many stops along the Chandernagor road, in the dead of night! I still recall the silence, the trees, the fireflies that swirled around us, drugging us into a stupor of happiness.

I particularly remember a night when the car broke down. The chauffeur and Mantu went to get tools from the neighbouring village and Narendra Sen dozed off. Chabu, Maitreyi and I set off to explore the forest. The moonless summer night was alight with all the stars of Bengal; fireflies descended on our faces, our shoulders, our necks, like the living jewels of some folk-tale. We did not speak. Little by little, Maitreyi and I moved closer to each other, frightened that Chabu might see us, but encouraged by the silence and the darkness. I do not know what unknown state of being awoke in me, in response to that undreamt-of India stretching out before me. The forest seemed without beginning, without end. The sky veiled itself behind ageless eucalyptus trees, the eye unable to distinguish between the fireflies and the tiny, faraway stars. We stopped at the edge of a pond, all three of us silent. What spells were being woven in those closed lotus petals, in that motionless, soundless water which reflected the flight of a thousand points of gold? Relentlessly, I forced myself to keep awake, to resist the enchantment of the fable that surrounded us. The rational being inside me was floundering in the unreality and the sanctity of our presence at the edge of that silent lake. The state of ecstasy lasted for what seemed an age. I did not speak. I would not have dared embrace Maitreyi, yet I did not feel, in any case, the need to make the slightest gesture. A miraculous tranquillity, that did not belong to this world – yet which manifested in me with a flaming power – inhabited me. I have never understood the mystery of those blessed moments...

On another occasion, we discovered a ruined house, overgrown with vegetation, at the edge of a paddy-field into which I had wandered. I had come back soaked to my knees and to dry myself I sat on a wall of the shack. The stars had not yet come out and the evening was warm, filled with the scent of eucalyptus. Seated near me, Maitreyi, dressed in a sari of some soft, diaphanous material, was looking out at the forest on the other side of the field. It was as though everything around us were encouraging our desire for solitude, for escape. The wood invited us into it by the thickness and shadiness of its trees and the joy of its birdsong. We looked at each other and the same indefinable emotion that we had felt in the library flooded over us. I helped her down from the wall, brushing my lips against her hair. Everything of the young man that I was at that moment was contained in that kiss. Maitreyi closed her eyes, abandoning herself to her feeling, forgetting for a moment the worry that continually haunted us: could "the others" see us?

Those walks have stayed fresh in my memory and their tenderness still torments me. Carnal memories of the intimacy of two bodies – even in the most perfect of unions – fade like the memory of hunger or thirst, but our communion on those trips outside the city did not have the fragility of sensual pleasures; we could express all that we wanted simply with our eyes. A

brief kiss in such moments had more meaning for us than a
night of passion. The thrill of those hypnotic, insatiable
exchanges of the eyes was our secret treasure. When the car
stopped at the town gates, in the full light, our eyes met and
locked in a feverish contemplation, a communion that was close
to insanity in its fervour. I do not know how that passion – so
different from the friendship for which they hoped – escaped
the notice of our companions.

I remember one night when we went through Chandernagor. The brilliant lights of the town as we drove back did
not erase the melancholy and weariness left in me after seeing
the ruins of the palace – a glorious souvenir of what had once
been, separated by half the world, a colony of France. I
reflected on the power and the timelessness of the India that
endures everything, heedless of the crowds that teem across it
and the powers that subjugate it. As I was swept along in a
modern car, I felt beside me the presence of an impenetrable,
incomprehensible soul, as chimerical and sacred as the soul of
that other Maitreyi, the solitary figure of the Upanishads. I
touched her arm to reassure myself of her reality. Was it truly
by this girl that I was loved?

We often went to Swami Vivekananda's ashram at Belur-
Math, especially when some celebration was being held there.
The Ganges laps the steps of the *math* and the surrounding
scenery, filled with fragrances, is magnificent. We would walk
freely about the ashram, speaking little and abstaining from
every gesture of love. I experienced a calm in that place that
I had known nowhere else.

Was it the strength of my passion or convictions that I had
already formed which gave me the idea of conversion? If I were
to embrace Hinduism, all obstacles to our marriage would be
swept away. I told Maitreyi of my plan at Belur-Math. She
stood, stupefied, for a moment and then declared that if I
converted, nothing and no one could separate us. That very
evening, as soon as we had returned to Bhowanipore, she told

her mother the news. Bursting with happiness, she came down to my room to tell me that Mrs Sen and the women were overcome with joy. I could now ask for her hand without fear. I would simply have to wait for the right moment. We embraced, secure and contented. Later, our confidence was to fill me with a sense of unease. Was this unanimous approval, this universal benevolence, not simply the portent of separation and destruction?

When he heard me speak of conversion, Narendra Sen was visibly angry. I should not hurl myself into a religion simply because I was charmed by its novelty and its curious rituals. My own religion was far superior to his. If he remained faithful to Hinduism, it was only because if he gave it up, he would lose his position in society. I had no such motive to consider.

This clear and powerful opposition plunged us into despondency. We decided that I would go and spend a month in Puri in October. I would come back converted and further argument would be impossible.

Narendra Sen, who had been suffering from high blood pressure for several months, had several attacks of 'moving flies' and the whole house was thrown into a state of alarm. Our outings in the car grew rare. I spent most of my time in the patient's room, reading him novels or books on psychology and medicine (condemned to immobility, he had begun to reflect on his soul and his illness; he wanted to educate himself on both subjects). Mantu, Maitreyi and I continually took turns in looking after him. He was not in pain, but he was forced to spend most of the day stretched out on his bed, his eyes protected by dark glasses.

I had not really been aware of his illness, so occupied, so fascinated had I been by our games and our love. I realized then that I had been oblivious to a whole host of events. Civil war was threatening to break out again, fuelled by the imprisonment of over 50,000 nationalists. I had to witness scenes of violence, charges by mounted police, the sacking and pillaging of the

Sikh district in Bhowanipore, I had to see children beaten and
women hurt before I, too, became caught up in the revolution.
In doing so, I lost my clarity of judgement. I condemned the
British out of hand and every new brutality reported by the
newspapers sent me into a rage; whenever I passed Europeans
in the street, I looked at them with disgust. I refused to buy
English goods: I would have only swadeshi products, although
the life I led at Bhowanipore meant I needed to buy very few
things – tobacco, a little toothpaste.

Several days after the attack on the Sikh district, Harold
came to see me. My prediction had been good: he wanted
another, larger, loan – 100 rupees this time. I had money in
the Chartered Bank and I gave him a cheque, both pleased to be
able to help him (the poor chap owed three months rent and
could not afford to eat until he was paid at the end of the month)
and furious at myself for helping an enemy of India. I was
becoming a chauvinist...

Maitreyi served us tea and stayed behind in my room for a
while. I was attempting to discuss Gandhi and the revolution
with Harold who, like all the Anglo-Indians, had ferocious
views on the subject. He was delighted by the violence
unleashed by the police and the army. However, he had just
borrowed money from me and he could not contradict me.
This discovery of his cowardice and hypocrisy – faults of
which I am myself so often guilty when I disagree with someone – saddened me. Harold had also come to spy on me, to
examine my lodgings, to see if I was, as he believed, leading the
life of a 'black savage' without comforts. Above all, he had come
to observe Maitreyi. When he saw her serving us tea, flushed
with shyness, giving me furtive little looks and smiles, saw how
at ease she was in my room and my company, he understood
everything.

"My dear Alain, you are hopelessly lost."

"It is my greatest wish to enter this world," I replied,
flushing with anger, looking him hard in the eyes. "It is a

world that is alive, with people who are alive, who suffer without complaint, who have not lost their sense of morality. Their young girls are saints, not prostitutes like ours. Do you think I would marry a white girl? A girl who has never truly been a virgin and who will never truly be a lover? The white world is a dead world. I have finished with it. If I am admitted, as I pray God I will be, into an Indian family, I will refashion my life. Until now, it has been based on stupid interests, on abstracts – I want to begin everything afresh, believe in something, be happy. Only a perfect love can make me happy and it is only here, in this place, in this house, that I can find such a love."

I had spoken with heat and sincerity, yet many of those ideas had never before entered my head. Harold looked at me, surprised, embarrassed, amused. He was at a loss for words. He had no idea what this 'death of the white world' – an idea that had obsessed me for months – meant. Besides, he was not inclined to discuss it. He wanted to hurry off to drink some of the whisky of which he had been deprived for so long.

"But your religion?" he asked, without much real interest.

"Christianity? It has its home here in India, in a nation that has the most serene relationship with God, where people thirst for love, for freedom, for intelligence. I cannot conceive of Christianity without freedom, without an essential spirituality..."

Until then, Harold had heard me speak about my work, my studies or my casual affairs. My eulogy to this new Hindu brand of Christianity was thus all the more astonishing to him. However, despite all my apparent enthusiasm, I myself was not completely convinced of the truth of all my fine sentiments, all my new-found political and religious beliefs; I had the feeling that they had their origin in my love for Maitreyi, nothing more.

I was to ask myself whether my emotional slavery had not determined all my actions. That was later, however, when I was

once more trying to get at the truth of our story. My God, yes!
The truth...

"I'm afraid that I don't understand you," said Harold. "May
the Lord keep you and protect you from evil!"

He got up, and left.

Still fired by my words, I paced my room, worrying that I had
not expressed all that I truly thought, when Maitreyi came in.
She kissed me.

"I am glad your friend has gone. I wanted so much to see
you..."

Holding her to me, I felt afraid for the first time that I would
one day tire of her love. I would have preferred to be alone, at
least for an hour or two, after Harold had left. His visit had
disturbed me and I wanted time to gather my thoughts, to put
them in order and draw conclusions. But no sooner had my
guest left than she had come to throw herself in my arms. I felt
as though some of my property had been stolen, my private
territory invaded. I had given myself completely to Maitreyi, I
was never apart from her; from the moment I woke until I fell
asleep, her image was with me. Why did she not sense when I
needed a little solitude? Why is the greatest love unable to
perceive the wishes of the beloved?

I held her in my arms, letting my lips fall softly on her
perfumed head. Suddenly, without warning, Khokha
entered, saw us and retreated, crying: "Sorry!"

XI

Coming back to my room later that day, I found a note on my table: "Come to the library!"

Maitreyi was waiting for me. She looked terrified.

"Khokha knows everything!" she blurted out.

I forced myself to appear calm and reassuring. She stared into my eyes intently, squeezing my hands tightly between hers, as though trying to make my confidence somehow flow into her.

"We must get engaged without saying anything to my father. He is ill. If we told him, it would make him worse."

"But surely we have been engaged for a long time? You gave me a garland, and we have kissed..."

"Yes, but Khokha has seen us. We must make our union even stronger. Otherwise, we will go against the Rhythm and we will be cursed..."

She looked all around her, as though terrified. I felt the same mixture of disillusionment and amusement that I always felt when I saw what a tangled growth of superstitions lay in Maitreyi's mind, in her love: Rhythm, Karma, Ancestors... How many Powers would have to be consulted and invoked if we were to be certain of happiness!

"I have chosen the stone for your ring."

She untied the corner of her sari and showed me a dark green jewel, engraved with a lizard's head and a border the colour of blood.

She explained its symbolism. It would be made of gold and iron and wrought, according to the rites of Hindu marriage, in the form of two intertwined snakes, one black and the other yellow, representing masculinity and femininity. She had chosen the stone from a large heap of similar jewels, amassed over generations, which Mrs Sen kept in a chest. The stone was valueless – and no one could say that she had stolen it by taking it without her mother's knowledge. Besides, there had been so many others in the chest. I wondered why she was excusing and defending herself in this way. She told me later that she had feared I would adopt a severe, "Christian" stance and reproach her in the name of morality.

An Indian engagement is not usually sanctioned in that way. It is the young girl who receives a bracelet with the interwoven strands of gold and iron on the inside. The young man wears only a simple band. But Maitreyi could not openly wear such a bracelet and so the two symbols had to be united in my jewel.

She spoke for a long time that evening and I listened, bewitched. Yet the little lucidity that I retained revolted against this bizarre ceremony, with its pretensions to mysticism. Every attempt to submit our love to a code of symbolic rules seemed a violation. I longed for spontaneity, for a free expression of love. All the same, when the jeweller brought me the ring, I took it in my hands and examined it minutely, with all the enthusiasm of a child. It had been engraved so skilfully that it might pass as a ring of no special significance – although certainly more original than most. At any rate, no one in the house guessed its meaning. Lilu and Mantu spoke of my future marriage to an Indian woman and accused me of wearing an engagement ring... but it was nothing more than teasing. In any case, the engineer was still ill. He had obtained extra leave and the household's sole preoccupation was in looking after him.

The next day, Maitreyi pretended that she was very tired and asked for the car to go to the lakes, at a time when she knew everyone would be busy. Only Chabu wanted to accompany us, but for several days she had not been well; she did not speak for long periods, would not say what was wrong, stared into space or sang nonsense to herself. Mrs Sen did not allow her to go out and gave us for companion one of Khokha's sisters, a timid young widow who worked like a slave and who never had the chance to go out in the car. I sat in the front seat next to the chauffeur and the two young women sat behind. When we arrived at the lakes, the woman stayed in the car, which had been parked near the road under a giant eucalyptus, the chauffeur went in search of lemonade and Maitreyi and I walked alone to the water's edge. I loved nothing in Calcutta so much as the lakes – the only artificial works in a town that had grown out of the jungle. They were as still as an aquarium and at night, by the light of the electric lamps, they looked as if they were made of glass. In my imagination, the park was without limits, even though I knew its boundaries perfectly well: the railway track on one side, the road and the suburbs on the other.

I liked to wander along the paths and to go down to the edge of the water where younger trees, planted after the lakes had been built, were growing in their own fashion and in their own time, like veritable individuals. It was as if they sensed a jungle had once been all-powerful in that place and wanted to restore some of that lost wilderness.

We stopped beneath one of those clumps of trees. We were completely hidden. Maitreyi took the ring from my finger and cradled it in her small hands.

"This is the moment of our engagement, Alain," she said, her eyes fixed on the distant water.

This solemn overture irritated me. I could not shake off my rationality towards her – and yet how I loved her! My God, how I loved her... I wondered what picturesque scene was about to unfold: it would be taken from one of those medieval Hindu ballads that tell of a legendry and fantastic love. I had the western superstition of common sense and horror of all "mystical" exaltation. And, like every civilized man, I – who believed I had eschewed civilization, torn it, roots and all, from my soul – became awkward and helpless before a solemn gesture to execute, a serious word to proclaim, a promise to give.

Maitreyi continued, however, with a simplicity that finally won me. She spoke to the water, to the star-filled sky, to the forest, to the earth. She pressed the grass hard with her clenched fists, which held the ring, and made her vow:

"I swear by you, Earth, that I will be Alain's and his alone. I will grow in him, like the earth grows in you. As you wait for rain, I will wait for him and his body will be like the rays of the sun to me. I swear in your presence that our union will be fertile, because I love him from my own free will. Let none of the harm that comes, if it comes, fall on him but on me alone, who chose him. You listen to me, Mama Earth, and you tell me the truth. If I am dear to you, as you are to me, this moment, with my hand, with the ring, give me the strength to love him forever, to give him a joy which others do not know, a life full of richness and joy. May our life be like the freshness of the grass which grows from you. May our embraces be like the first day of the monsoon. May our kisses be like the rain. As you never get tired, my sweet Mama, may my heart never tire of its love for Alain... whom the Sky gave birth to far away but who you, little mother, have brought so close to me..."

I listened to her, increasingly entranced, until her words became unintelligible. She was speaking a simplified, childish Bengali, almost lisping the words... I heard the sounds, I understood a word here and there but I could not catch the meaning of the incantation that followed. When finally she fell silent, I felt almost frightened to touch her, she seemed so spell-bound, so inaccessible. I knelt by her side, one hand pressing against the earth, as though I too were taking an oath, caught by the magical power of the gesture.

It was she who broke the silence.

"Now no one can ever separate us, Alain. Now I am yours, totally yours..."

I caressed her, searching for words that I had never spoken to

her, but I could find nothing new, nothing which did justice to
my inner fever and her transfigured face. In that moment, she
was someone I did not know, could not touch. The memory of
the strange, fixed expression of her face would stay with me for
a long time. That evening – and it was the only time – I did not
kiss her. Finally, the moment was broken.

"One day you will marry me and show me to the world?"

She had spoken in English, and reddened at the crude turn
of phrase she had used.

"My English is very bad, Alain. Who knows what disagreeable things you must have understood. I mean that I would like
to see the world with you, see it as you see it yourself. It is big
and beautiful, isn't it? Why do men fight everywhere? I would
like them all to be happy. No, I am talking nonsense. How I love
the world as it is! How I love it!"

She began to laugh. Suddenly she had become the Maitreyi
of the winter before, an innocent, shy child, saying whatever
came into her head, delighting in paradox. Every trace of the
experience that had matured her, made her conscious of herself
and almost transformed her into a woman, seemed to have
disappeared. Indeed, in the days that followed, it became clear
that our engagement had restored her calm and her love of
games, of spontaneous joy. From the moment she had sworn
our union, she was no longer tormented by fear of fainting or
the obsession that she was committing a sin. I rediscovered the
intriguing, elusive Maitreyi of our earliest days, the girl whom I
had contemplated with wonder and amazement and who had
entered my heart before I had realized it. In the ridiculous traps
that I had set for her, I had succeeded in catching only myself.

It was already pitch dark and we returned to the car quickly.
We walked back slowly, side by side. We must have made a fine
couple: I taller than Maitreyi, she younger, and so incredibly
beautiful. We found our companion dozing on the back seat,
her shawl pulled up over her head. When she saw us, she gave a
shy, conspiratorial smile.

Maitreyi told me, later, that Khokha's sister had been the first person she had told of our love; the widow had done all that she could to protect her. That woman, who had suffered so much from a badly arranged marriage – at the age of twelve, she had been married to a man who had terrorized her: he had brutally raped her and he beat her every night, before and after having sex with her – had continually advised Maitreyi not to let herself be intimidated by the laws of caste and family but to act on her feelings. If our love met with forceful opposition, she should run away with me. She was my ally and Maitreyi's confidante, yet I rarely saw her and spoke to her only by chance. I do not know what she was called. I have looked through my diary several times to discover her name. It is not mentioned.

That night, Chabu got worse and Mrs Sen took her to sleep with her in her own room. No one knew what the matter was. The symptoms were worrying: she tried constantly to lean out of the window or the balcony. She thought she could see something down there, in the street, calling to her. I went to bed tired by the day's events. I must have dreamed strange things, of walking on water, of swans and fireflies, for when I awoke with a start, at the sound of knocking on my door, my mind was wild and confused. I asked who was there – no one answered. I confess I was frightened; I lit the lamp. The fan was turning and I listened to its whirring, a sound that one does not usually notice until it has stopped. Then, I opened the door and stood rooted to the spot with amazement. It was Maitreyi. She stood there, trembling all over, bare foot, wearing a sari of palest green. I stared at her, dumb, stupefied. I had no idea what to do.

"Turn out the light," she whispered, coming into the room, then ran to hide herself behind my armchair, fearing she would be seen from outside.

I turned it out, and moved towards her.

"What's the matter? Why are you here? What is wrong, Maitreyi?"

She did not reply but undid the edge of her sari, baring herself to the waist: her eyes were closed, her lips tensed. With great effort, she held back her sighs. The sight of her naked flesh, bathed in the soft light that filled my room, seemed to me an unsurpassed miracle. I had often pictured our first night of love, I had conjured up in my imagination the bed, transfigured by desire, where I would know her, but I could never have dreamed that Maitreyi, of her own free will, would reveal her young body to me, in my own room, at night. I had wanted our union to be breath-taking, to take place in extraordinary circumstances, but this spontaneous gesture exceeded my every hope.

I was struck by the simplicity, the naturalness of the initiative taken by a young virgin in coming alone at night into the bedroom of her fiancé because nothing more stood in the way of their union.

Very gently, I took her in my arms, fearing at first that I had come too close, naked as she was. Then, my hands brushed against the sari that covered her hips. With a single movement, I slid it down to her feet. I trembled at the sacrilege I had committed and knelt before that body whose nakedness seemed to surpass all human beauty, to partake in the divine. She put her arms around my shoulders, beseeching me silently to get up. Her whole body was quivering. Her happiness at our engagement – the happiness that had brought her here – could not obliterate the fear and the confusion of that moment. With light, supple steps, she walked to the bed, her entire body moving with a new rhythm. I wanted to take her in my arms to help her but she refused and lay down herself, covering my pillow with kisses. For an instant, stretched out on my white sheet, she resembled a bronze statue. She shivered, and breathlessly repeated my name. I pulled down the wooden shutters and our room was enveloped in darkness. She pressed tightly against my body as though she wanted to hide, to lose herself in me. It was no longer erotic desire, but a desperate longing for my whole being, for her flesh to be united with my flesh, just as her soul was already united with mine.

I remember nothing more, afterwards. I took her, blindly, and no trace of the memory has remained. Several hours later, as dawn approached, she got up and without looking at me, put on her sari. As she went through the door that I had opened to her so cautiously, with such a pounding heart, she said simply:

"Our union was ordained by the Sky. Today, the day of the ring, Chabu did not sleep with me."

I tried to follow the noise of her feet on the steps of the staircase that led to her room, but I heard nothing, so lightly did she pass along the length of the corridor.

In the morning, it was she who came to call me for tea. She had brought flowers from the garden. As she arranged them in vases, she gave me a smile whose warmth caressed me. The pallor of her face struck me. Her hair fell wildly over her shoulders: she told me later that I had ruffled it so much that she had been unable to comb out the knots. Her lips were covered in bite-marks and her full, finely drawn lower lip bore the marks of my lacerations like so many signs of conquest that both troubled and fascinated me. As I contemplated the traces of our first night of love, a nameless bliss flooded over me: she was beautiful, with a seductive beauty bordering on voluptuousness. It was as though her whole body had been awakened.

I wondered how her metamorphosis had gone unnoticed. Apparently, her explanations had been readily accepted... She had pretended that she had been so worried about Chabu and so exhausted by her father's illness that she could not sleep and had wept all night, biting her lips until they bled.

The day passed quickly. I spent it entirely in the office, working with Narendra Sen's replacement. On my return, Maitreyi was waiting for me on the veranda, near the letter box. She showed me a ring that she had made for herself by twisting a hair pin around her finger. In place of a stone it held a bud of wisteria.

"Don't bolt your door at night," she said, and disappeared.

She came to me around midnight; this time, she was not trembling. As she kissed me, she was almost laughing. I was happy that she was not troubled by what she had done, that she was free of any notion of sin.

She was a different being, so ardent was her desire, so sincere, so perfect her caresses. I was astonished that a woman who had been a virgin the night before could now display so much art. I felt certain that nothing would embarrass her, even though she herself did not make, even accidentally, any gesture of the slightest immodesty or lewdness.

She discovered herself in our love-making. We had taken to our games again, and she played them whole-heartedly, giving herself without restriction or fear. This young girl, who know nothing of love, had no fear of it; no caress tired her, no male gesture offended her. She knew every audacity, every tenderness. She had almost nothing of prudery, finding a total sensuality in each posture, feeling neither disgust nor fatigue. If she had not been afraid of being heard, she would have shouted with pain and pleasure at the moment of our union, she would have sung afterwards, she would have danced across the room with the light and delicate movements of a little goddess.

She discovered lover's gestures that astounded me. I had believed that my experience granted me some superiority in the art of loving, but in the invention and execution of caresses she was the expert. I found the confidence of her kisses, the perfection of her embraces, the changing, intoxicating rhythms of her body – which were at every moment more daring, more original, more spontaneous – disconcerting, almost humiliating. She understood the tiniest hint, followed every initiative to its conclusion. I was envious of her instinct. She divined my physical desires with a precision that at first embarrassed me. The very second I wanted to be left alone, simply to lie beside her, touching only her hand, she sensed it and very quietly drew away from me, as though for a moment of rest. While I lay

there, reflecting, she would bury herself in my pillow, kiss it
and close her eyes.

I had found a little bedside lamp and I placed it, covered with
Maitreyi's shawl, behind the armchair. Under that dimmed
light, the curvature of the bronze body became purer and its
rounded forms glistened in the shadows. Maitreyi had not
tolerated darkness for long: in her passion, she wanted to
possess me with her eyes also.

I often wondered when she managed to sleep. She always left
at dawn. For two or three hours she would meditate, write – to
give me the joy of reading, the next day at the office, poems and
letters that sang of our love. And then she would come down to
prepare the tea. It was she who, discreet and cautious, now
knocked at my door in the morning. If I lingered over my
ablutions, she scolded me as though I were a child. Her voice
would take on a familiar, protective, maternal tone which
irritated me at first – I wanted her as lover, nothing else –
but then began to charm me. I was discovering depths and
varieties of love that I had hitherto condemned out of hand,
not realizing their tenderness.

I was constantly tired in the afternoons and I did not work
well at the office; my new superior humiliated me and I felt
nothing but contempt for him. He had lived in America and
now spurned Indian traditions; although a Bengali, he wore
European clothes, even at home. He was totally ridiculous.

With his unfailing accuracy, Khokha observed the change in
me.

"You are very pale. Why do you sleep with the shutters
closed?"

I understood from that question that, from spite and jealousy, Khokha was spying on us. I was certain then that he
knew of Maitreyi's nocturnal visits to my room and I was afraid
he would denounce us. I began being very friendly towards
him: I bought him cigarettes, gave him books... He was an
intelligent and ambitious young man, who wrote scripts –

which were regularly rejected – for Indian film companies. He despised us all, even though he was forever laughing with everyone, feigning affection.

Chabu was getting worse. The doctors – first Indians and then the most renowned English specialists – were at a loss. Some diagnosed *dementia praecox*. Others believed it was hysteria. She was confined to the little room adjoining Mrs Sen's. She rarely spoke, and when she did it was only to ramble in her delirium about Robi Thakkur or the path visible from Maitreyi's room. If she was left alone, she would escape on to the balcony and stare down at the path, sing, gesticulate with her arms, cry – and so she was continually watched over by Lilu or by Khokha's sisters. Strangely, she recognized only Maitreyi and me, very seldom her mother.

I wondered how poor Mrs Sen managed to keep her calm and her smile: her husband was in severe pain, her daughter was going mad. How could she look after everything that happened in that huge house, watch over each one of us, serve meals or tea punctually? I upbraided myself sincerely for spending my nights with Maitreyi during that time. I looked forward with impatience to the day when Mrs Sen would learn of our folly, and forgive us. My trip to Puri, to convert, had been postponed because of the engineer's illness. Besides, Maitreyi did not want me to go and Mrs Sen feared for my safety – the political unrest in southern Bengal was growing increasingly bloody.

One day, Chabu caught sight of my ring and asked if she could play with it. I hesitated. I had promised Maitreyi that I would never take it off, not even for a moment. I looked at her, silently asking her what I should do. She had to agree. Chabu was crying and demanding the ring. When the child had it in her hands, she stared at it, rolled it between her fingers, tried to look through it, then rolled it in a handkerchief and cradled it to her neck. I do not know what it was in the black stone that attracted her.

The doctors could do nothing for her madness and the wizards and the magicians were once again called in. An uncle of the girls also came, a very gentle old man who radiated an atmosphere of calm. He played vaishnava hymns all day, heart-rending, cruel songs that weakened the will and plunged the soul into melancholy. The whole household came to listen to him, Narendra Sen laid out on a couch, a pillow behind his head and dark glasses protecting his eyes, Mantu, Khokha and I seated on the ground with the women. A curious thing then happened. A tide of emotion swept over them all; even the engineer wept. Maitreyi hid her face in her shawl, sighing. Appalled by this collective passion, I got up to leave. But the kirtan reached every corner of the house and even in my room I was not free of it. In my solitude, the plaintive song disturbed me even more.

Her uncle tried to soothe Chabu's mind by another method. He had brought with him some traditional medicine: a paste made from herbs and honey. The ointment had to be smeared on the little patient's head, directly on to the scalp. A painful scene ensued. No one had the courage to cut Chabu's hair and I was charged with the task. I stroked her forehead and, looking her straight in the eyes, chopped off hunks of her hair. I talked to her continually, so that she would not hear the sound of the scissors, while Maitreyi, standing behind the bed, caught the locks and hid them in a veil. When the top of Chabu's head was exposed, Mrs Sen applied the still warm mixture. Chabu looked at us, tried to feel her scalp, and then took the hand-kerchief, with the ring inside, from her neck and began crying softly. Her tears fell abundantly on to her beautiful dark face. No sigh, no sob came from her. Perhaps she had understood she was half bald. I do not know. She was often overcome by such sudden fits of crying, especially when she was prevented from getting up to look out of the window.

The days passed in an atmosphere of extreme agitation. I would come back from the office, go upstairs to have news of the engineer and of Chabu, wash, eat and then take up my post at the little girl's bedside. She often called for me in her delirium and would become a little calmer when I was near her.

I spent every night with Maitreyi. She desired me with ever greater sincerity and ardour and that intensity was fuelled by her terror at all the events taking place around us. She would give herself to me with a crazed passion. I would awake in the mornings exhausted, filled with an indefinable fear. Narendra Sen continually postponed the date of the operation on his eyes. The doctors had recommended total rest for him and the atmosphere of foreboding that hung over the house, caused by all the events taking place in it, hardly improved his chances of recovery. I was frightened we would betray ourselves by some carelessness. Maitreyi worried me. She came to me at night, before the rest of the house was fully asleep. In Chabu's room, she squeezed my arm, leaned against my shoulder with the whole weight of her body, kissed my hand – when she might be seen at any moment. Moreover, Khokha had surprised us kissing countless times and Lilu and Mantu strongly suspected a relationship between us, although they would never have dreamed that we were lover and mistress. Maitreyi sometimes behaved in ways that I did not understand, that tormented me and threw me into appalling fits of doubt. She had suffered from beri-beri and at night her legs swelled slightly; in very hot weather, the doctors had advised massages for her. On such days, in the morning, Lilu or Khokha's sisters would massage her naked body with some revolting oil that was almost impossible to remove afterwards, even with copious washing. She was sometimes afflicted by sudden sharp pains in her legs and had to be massaged immediately. Since it was only her legs that were affected, Khokha was able to massage her and, to my annoyance, she would call him into her room to perform the task.

I reproved her for it one day; she looked at me, stupefied, and replied that I could hardly expect to be called myself for such a disagreeable job, a job that the masseurs were paid to do. Perhaps, but Khokha was not a professional masseur, he was young, he made her laugh and I shook with rage at the thought of those huge, black hands greedily pawing Maitreyi's flesh.

One evening, she called Khokha from the inner balcony. She was in great pain: it had been raining for two days. Khokha was not at home and so she called for the chauffeur instead. I almost lost my head and ran to her room, to hurl stinging reproaches at her, but I was suddenly ashamed of my fantasies. I was not ashamed, however, a few moments later, of hiding myself in the garden to spy on her. She had not yet lit her lamp, as – I reflected bitterly – she should have done, from modesty and love for me. I imagined a whole panoply of disgusting images, I recalled episodes from cheap novels in which the chauffeur becomes his mistress's lover, I thought of all the cynical aphorisms about female infidelity and the fundamental treachery of woman. A thousand tiny details, insignificant until then, sprang to mind: one day, Mantu had locked himself into Maitreyi's room and from below, I had heard a struggle, angry shouting. It had sounded like a street brawl. When they emerged from the room, Mantu looked wild and flushed, Maitreyi deathly pale, her hair falling dishevelled around her shoulders. It is true that she herself had told me, just before the incident, that Mantu was ignoble, that he had tried to touch her intimately and that she had slapped him and complained to her father. But Narendra Sen was ill and Mantu had made himself indispensable. It would have been impossible to throw him out.

I also remembered that she had told me another of her uncles had tried to kiss her breasts and to take her in his arms. But on that occasion the engineer had taken swift action. The wretched man must have regretted his lust – he was fired from his job and had to return to his village, where he led a cur's life. Maitreyi often complained about this carnal passion that she inspired in men, even blood relations. She suffered deeply because of it. She would have preferred to inspire around

her something other than a frustrated sexual desire. Yet more
scenes rushed through my head: one evening, for example,
Khokha had detained Maitreyi for a long time on the veranda. On joining us for dinner, she was agitated and nervous.
He did not dare show himself.

All those incidents tortured me. It seemed that every man
desired Maitreyi and that she gave herself to all of them. Why
else did the chauffeur spy on us, if it were not because he
wanted her, because he was planning to risk everything one
day and to burst in on her in her room, ready to leave that night,
without his wages? I imagined such absurdities and I suffered
agonies of torture: my jealousy would not spare me the tiniest
detail. I could not shake myself free from that pathological
obsession: Maitreyi in other men's arms.

I came in from the garden, mortally wounded. During dinner, I kept my legs under my chair. When I went to bed, I put
the large wooden bolt on the floor, determined, no matter what,
that I would not open it to Maitreyi. I was still awake when she
came to the door: I pretended I was asleep and had not heard
her. She began knocking loudly, calling my name and then
shaking the door violently. I was afraid that someone would
hear her and finally I succumbed.

"Why did you bolt the door? Do you not want me any
more?"

She was pale, crying and shaking. I closed the door and we
sat on my bed. Resisting the urge to kiss her, I explained my
torment to her. She put her arm around me and covered me
with feverish kisses, digging her nails into my flesh. I went on
speaking, making myself insensible to the warmth of her body.
I told her the suffering of knowing she was alone with a stranger
who was massaging her legs. I told her how hideous that
abandonment to a man's hands was to me.

"I am sorry he did not rape me!" she burst out and began
sobbing.

"With you, sensual and immoral as you are, it would have

been an easy task!" I replied, throwing her a look of hatred. "You love the idea of such improbable affairs, such primitive, grotesque conquests – that are, in fact, incredibly banal – which that old snake, your so-called spiritual master, stuffed into your head for so long."

I got up and began pacing the room, showering her with cruel insults, humiliating her with every word. I hated her, despised her – not because she had been unfaithful but because she had made me believe blindly in her love, her purity, had made me a laughing stock by forcing me to give her everything, to take on her desires and her will as my own. The idea that I had given my entire being to a child who would fall into the arms of any passer-by enraged me.

In fact, I did not believe she would betray me, but I was caught in the mesh of my own fury. At that moment, it was as though everything she had ever done or said had been nothing but hypocrisy. I could not have had such suspicions of a white woman. I knew well the superficiality and capriciousness of our women, but I also knew that a certain self-respect and sense of moderation would have stopped them giving themselves to the merest stranger. Maitreyi was still an enigma to me. I could not predict her actions. It seemed to me that, primitive and irrational as she was, she could have given herself to someone without even suspecting the seriousness of her actions and without assuming responsibility for them. My jealousy had been transformed into hatred and I forgot all that I had experienced over the past few months. I forgot Maitreyi's innocence and her almost supernatural purity: all I could see was fantastic treachery.

I understood then the fragility of human feelings. The most solid confidence can be broken by a single gesture. Sexual possession – even that obtained in the most perfect trust – is hardly effective proof of loyalty. Cannot that same sincerity be offered to another, to others? My blissful happiness and the confidence that had been accumulated over so many months of love, over so many nights spent together, were as nothing. As though banished by some spell, they had ceased to exist. All that remained in me was an overblown male pride and a terrible rage against myself.

I could see that Maitreyi was suffering as she listened to my invective – and that exasperated me still more. She bit her lips until they were bloody, looked at me with huge, astonished eyes, as though she doubted the reality of what was happening.

"But what did I say, my God, what did I say?" she burst out suddenly.

"You talked of rape!"

"Why do you not want to understand? Why do you prefer to be disgusted by me than to understand? You have forgotten everything. You told me one day that if I were raped and thrown out of the house, you would still love me. I said to myself that if such a thing happened, I would be happy. There would be no more obstacles to our marriage. Alain, believe me, we cannot marry – and we will die with this crime on our souls! Even if you convert, they would never accept you as my husband! They expect something else from you. Have you forgotten? But if someone disgraced me, they would have to throw me on to the street or the sin would fall on the whole house. If I were rejected by them, we could marry, I could become a Christian. It is not a sin for a Christian to be raped against her will and you would still love me. Is it true that you would still love me? Tell me, Alain – tell me. You would not forget me? You know what will happen to me if you forget me."

I was, I have to confess, moved. I felt as though I were waking from a nightmare; my fury had dissolved and I bitterly regretted my words. I wanted to ask her forgiveness, but I could foresee the scene of reconciliation and it was false, ridiculous, revolting.

I did not know what to do and I looked at her, trying to express all my repentance and my love with my eyes. But she was weeping too violently, she was too distraught, to see my shame. She threw herself at my feet, clasping my knees, asking if I had grown tired of her love, if I were frightened by the sin we had committed... Today, those questions seem naïve, but at the time they seared me like fire. I took her in my arms and told her, by means of my caresses and my broken words, that I loved her as strongly as ever. I think she realized how much pain my own blindness had caused me.

We both avoided speaking of our marriage again that night. Things were no longer as simple as they had once seemed and I did not want to torment myself with an unreal hope. I almost preferred to accept that we would one day have to part.

There was a sound of footsteps outside the window. We stopped talking and turned out the light. The steps moved towards the veranda. Then, someone knocked on the door of the corridor. We both froze with terror. The knocking stopped, then began again on my shutters. I knew it must be Khokha, doubtless returning from a night at the local cinema. I went to open the door, pretending that I was having difficulty in unbolting it, to give Maitreyi time to return to her room.

"Were you talking to someone?" he asked insolently.

"No!" I replied savagely and slammed the door.

Then I heard, from the parallel corridor, outside Maitreyi's room, the voice of Mrs Sen.

XII

I thought they must have found out everything. I threw myself on to the bed and lay there, unable to sleep. At dawn, Maitreyi came to my room, soundlessly, and slipped a note under the door.

"Mama knows nothing. Do not worry. Do not give yourself away."

It was as though some grace had been accorded me, as though my fate were being postponed. I wrote Maitreyi a long letter: we should put an end to these foolhardy meetings at night, when everyone was still up, looking after the engineer or Chabu. In truth, I no longer knew how we could end our affair. To see her mother's reaction, Maitreyi had told her one day that I was madly in love with one of her friends (we had christened her Anasuya: it was at the time that we were reading and studying "Shakuntala" together) and that I did not know how to ask for the young woman's hand in marriage. Mrs Sen had replied that such marriages are born of nothing more than sentimental fantasy, could lead only to unhappiness for both husband and wife and that no lasting happiness could result from a passion that is not tempered by tradition – in other words, by the family, people who knew that love and marriage are much more serious than we young people realized. To marry did not mean picking flowers together nor did it mean allowing oneself to be consumed by an ephemeral, misleading passion.

I admit that I recognized myself in all that. Our love was nothing other than passion; we had thought only of ourselves.

Mrs Sen had added that marriage was never founded on love alone, but on sacrifice, renunciation, the complete acceptance of the will of fate – and such a philosophy, despite my sincere allegiance to India, I could never adopt.

I understood then what insurmountable obstacles stood in the way of my desire to marry Maitreyi. I even asked myself if her wild solution – rape – would not be the most effective. Her parents would be presented with a fait accompli, would be forced to accept me as son-in-law – no one else would marry their daughter. It is hard for me to appreciate, today, how precious Maitreyi must have been to me for me to have contemplated such a fantastic expedient.

The days passed, repeating themselves in their terrors and in the increasingly dangerous risks we were taking. I was so absorbed in all these events that I never took time to contemplate them, to record them in detail: my notes for that period are so scanty that they seem to me like the fragments of someone else's life.

One event stands out among those days and nights of torment: Maitreyi's birthday on September 10th. Despite his illness and Chabu's delirium, the engineer wanted to celebrate it in great style. Maitreyi would be seventeen and that age possessed some esoteric significance in India. Her volume of poetry, *Uddhita*, published several days earlier, had been ecstatically received by the critics and Narendra Sen planned to invite all the literary and artistic élite of Calcutta, to a function which he hoped would be a kind of artistic "tournament". The brightest luminaries of Calcutta – except Tagore who was in Europe – would be there, including Chatterji, the author of *Srikantha* and the dancer Udaj Shankar. I had for a long time been jealous of Shankar's god-like beauty, his fascinating sense of rhythm. We had attended one of his festivals in August; Maitreyi had completely forgotten my existence as she sat gazing at him as though in a trance, utterly conquered. For several days afterwards, she had spoken of nothing but him.

She desperately wanted to meet him, to learn, she said, the "secret of dance". The editors of the review *Prabuddha Bharatta* were also expected. Maitreyi counted numerous of her admirers among them – Acintya, for example, a very original, hotly discussed poet: he had just published a novel similar to James Joyce's *Ulysses* and as a consequence he now had the whole pleiade of elderly Bengali writers ranged against him.

I was somewhat intimidated by the preparations for the event. I knew that Maitreyi would belong to me less than ever on that day, that she would try, proud and coquettish as she was, to seduce all her guests. She did not stay long in my room the night before, she was so exhausted by all the preparations. The women had worked tirelessly: the steps and the walls of the staircase had been covered with antique carpets, vases of flowers had been placed everywhere, two rooms on the first floor had been cleared for the guests and two enormous divans had been created for them to sit on, bare-foot, by covering mattresses with shawls. While she had been decorating the staircase with old pictures, Maitreyi had accidently dropped a magnificent portrait of Tagore, given to her by the poet himself, with a dedication. The incident troubled her: the frame had splintered into tiny pieces and the canvas was all torn, but more than that she saw it as a very bad omen.

I found her in the library at daybreak. I gave her my books, each with an innocuous dedication, and I kissed her, wishing her a peaceful life and all the happiness she deserved. As I spoke these few platitudes, my eyes filled with tears. She seemed distant, however. She freed herself from my arms and spoke to me far more casually than usual.

In the afternoon, I had to take part in the huge pantomime. I was again wearing a Bengali costume of silk and I looked after all those illustrious personages like a real Indian host – the engineer was immobilized in his armchair, the only piece of furniture in the room. All the guests were seated on the divans.

Mrs Sen and the other women of the house looked after the ladies, who remained out of sight in the neighbouring room, while Mantu stood in the ground floor corridor, acting as guide for the new arrivals.

Maitreyi was the only woman who came into our room, distributing copies of her *Uddhitha* and adding some softness to the atmosphere. I saw all those men drinking her in with their eyes, desiring her: she looked wonderful, with her soft pallor and her graceful charm. She was wearing a blue silk sari, her arms bare. I was in agonies. They were all indulging in a thousand dreams and plans – none of them knew that she was mine, mine alone. The beautiful Udaj Shankar made his entrance. Close to, he was less beautiful than on stage – yet he was still the most captivating man I had ever seen. His body was manly, but graced with an astonishing elasticity. His gestures, his expressions, had a softness that was entirely feminine – without being in any way freakish – and at the same time an extraordinary warmth and power of attraction. Maitreyi flushed as soon as she saw him. She took him out on to the balcony to get something to eat; the other visitors pressed around him so closely that he was unable to swallow a mouthful.

I tried to hide my unease. This magnificent dancer was much more than an attractive man. I sensed in him a magical power of seduction which could have conquered the entire female population of the city, let alone a girl such as Maitreyi – already in love and easily swayed. I knew that no one could resist him and I envied him that gift. But I did not hate him. I would have been happy if Maitreyi's expression had betrayed her feelings for him – at a single blow, I would have been cut free of my attachment. The instant I knew myself replaced by another, my love would have dissolved. If Maitreyi could not arm herself against Udaj Shankar's power with her fidelity to me, she deserved to be abandoned, like the most wretched of women.

I left the room and saw Maitreyi sitting in the corridor, next to Shankar. Fearfully, she was asking him questions which I could not make out. I was astounded by the calmness with which I contemplated them. Several moments later I found myself face to face with Maitreyi on the staircase. She squeezed my arm discreetly and said:

"I tried to find out the secret of dance from Shankar but he could not tell me anything. He is an idiot. He does not understand rhythm. He talks as though he is reciting lines. We should not have invited him. At the festival, he danced like a god but when I questioned him he only mumbled nonsense, like some vulgar peasant... How can dance not have made him intelligent?"

I could not thank her enough for those few words. She led me into the library and said, with fervour, caressing my hand:

"I love you, Alain, I love you more and more..."

I wanted to take her in my arms but we suddenly heard a loud noise coming from the floor above. Mrs Sen was calling her and the other women were shouting with terror.

We ran, both seized with a terrible fear, as if we had the foreboding of catastrophe. We found several of the women restraining Chabu, who was struggling and trying to jump down into the street. On this day of general chaos, the poor child had been left almost entirely alone. She had put on her best sari, which made her look older – ordinarily, she wore short dresses, in the European style – and had taken it into her head that she was going to attend the party. But when she set foot in the corridor, she saw the crowds of people and took fright. She ran on to the balcony where Shankar had been a few minutes before and leaned out to look at the street, singing, as was her custom. Two women had caught sight of her as she was climbing over the balustrade and had rushed to pull her back.

She was struggling wildly. The corridor filled with people and the engineer lost his composure, berating his wife savagely. I myself had to take Chabu in my arms and carry her like a small child into her room. She had recognized me at once. She pressed herself against my chest, crying and shouting, "Alain! Alain!" As I was putting her to bed, she suddenly asked me, her face grave:

"Maitreyi? Do they want to sell her?"

The next day, everyone was exhausted by the big occasion. It had cost nearly 500 rupees and had demanded much work. There had been speeches, a lavish meal on the terrace and Maitreyi had received numerous gifts, mostly books. The morning of the festivities, someone had sent her an enormous bunch of flowers, accompanied by an envelope. When she saw the handwriting, she looked uneasy, and read the letter rapidly, fearing she would be seen. Hearing footsteps on the staircase, she took refuge in my room. She handed me the envelope.

"Hide it in your desk and make sure no one sees it. I will take it later," she added, blushing.

I was bewildered, although I had no reason to worry: she had entrusted me with a letter in Bengali, that I could easily have deciphered or have asked a friend to translate for me. I did wonder what admirer had sent her the flowers and why Maitreyi had lied to her mother, telling her they came from a school friend who was unable to attend...

The days and the nights continued to pass – not many, however, because a week after her birthday the storm broke. I should be able to recount that last, brief period in detail, yet my notes contain nothing but the sketchiest outline of my life. The terse entries give no indication of impending catastrophe. It is strange that I have never been able to foresee my immediate future...

Every evening, we went to the lakes and sometimes we took Chabu. The engineer himself encouraged us to relax: we had exhausted ourselves looking after the patients. It was true that Maitreyi was growing frail. Chabu had become calmer, after her fit on Maitreyi's birthday, but she too needed walks in the

fresh air, after spending hours in her room. We would leave at
dusk and did not return until nine or ten o'clock. Chabu, sitting
on a bench or on the bank of the river, would barely speak but
stared into the distance, singing to herself or crying. We sat
close to her, talking and kissing surreptitiously. Maitreyi
repeated obsessively:

"One day you will take me all over the world. You will show
me the world."

She thought seriously about running away, especially when I
told her that I had a fair amount saved in the bank. I spent
almost nothing of my monthly salary of 400 rupees.

On the evening of September 16th, as we sat looking at the
lakes, Chabu became distraught and I carried her to the bench
and lay her down. We sat next to her, stroking her, speaking to
her affectionately and trying to make her laugh. She had taken
to laughing for no reason over the previous few days and the
doctors thought these fits of amusement were good for her.

"Why don't you like Alain?" she suddenly asked her sister.

We almost laughed ourselves, then. Chabu often talked
nonsense and we did not take her seriously.

"But I like him a lot!" replied Maitreyi, smiling.

"If you like him, kiss him!"

Maitreyi began laughing and said that a good little girl like
her should not say such silly things.

"Love is not silly," said Chabu, gravely. "Go on, kiss him.
Look, like this..."

She sat up and kissed me on the cheek. Maitreyi, still laughing, kissed me on the other.

"Are you happy now?" she asked.

"You, you should kiss him on the mouth!"

"Now, now, don't be silly," scolded Maitreyi, flushed with
embarrassment.

I was happy that my little sister Chabu, of whom I was so
fond, had noticed our love, and I asked Maitreyi to let me kiss
her on the lips. She refused. I slipped my hand beneath her

shawl and caressed her left breast, pressing my hand hard
against her, to hear the beating of her heart. I knew that I
was forcing her to kiss me: Maitreyi could never bear that
kind of caress without falling into my arms. At that moment,
Chabu also went to place her hand on Maitreyi's chest in an
affectionate gesture of insistence. Her hand met mine: I withdrew it at once, but it was too late. She began laughing and cried
triumphantly:

"Did you see, Alain put his hand on your chest?"

"Don't talk nonsense. It was my hand," replied Maitreyi
crisply.

"As if I didn't know! As if I had not felt Alain's ring!..."

So much precision surprised me. However, I was not frightened that the incident would have any serious consequences.

It was already dark and we returned to the car. By the time we
arrived back at the house, we had completely forgotten Chabu's
chatter.

That night, Maitreyi did not come to my room – just in case,
she said.

I can remember nothing of the next day. At six o'clock in the
evening, I put on my Bengal clothes and waited to be called for
the car to go to the lakes. No one came. A little irritated, I asked
the chauffeur if we were not going out that evening. He replied
in a tone that seemed to me insolent – although I may have been
mistaken – that he had been ordered to put the car in the
garage. Several moments later, I met Lilu in the corridor.
She announced that Mrs Sen had forbidden both Maitreyi
and Chabu to go walking around the lakes. I felt shrouded in
a mystery that I had, urgently, to break. I tried to find Maitreyi,
without success. Tormented with worry, I went back to my
room. A servant – instead of a member of the household, as
usual – came to call me for dinner. Only Mrs Sen and Maitreyi
were at the table. They did not speak. I tried to seem calm and
nonchalant – I believe I was marvellously successful. Mrs Sen
looked me straight in the eyes. I did not flinch from that steady

scrutiny, which penetrated me as though to reach my very soul. Her face had taken on an astounding air of concentration, a mocking smile played around her lips – reddened as usual with pan stains. She served me silently, politely, and then sat down again, her elbows on the table, observing me. Perhaps she was wondering how I had managed to deceive her for so long, under a guise of innocence and respect. I sensed beneath her hostile, ironic attitude the question she was asking herself, again and again: how could he have acted like this? – although I did not know exactly what that 'like this' consisted of in her mind. I was careful to appear calm and unruffled. I spoke naturally, I looked her in the eyes, I asked her how Mr Sen was and why the others had not come to dinner – I behaved as though there were absolutely nothing amiss.

Maitreyi squeezed my legs between hers as though she wanted to break them, expressing in that embrace all her final passion and terror. Then, with a gentleness I had never known in her before, her warm skin rubbed softly against mine. Her last caress infused me with a warmth and a passion that I will never forget, separated though we are in time and in distance...

Mrs Sen was called away from the upper floor and as soon as we were alone, Maitreyi said to me, biting her lips to control her feelings:

"Chabu has told Mama everything. But I have denied it. Do not worry. I am still yours. If they question you, admit nothing. Otherwise, who knows?"

She began weeping and was about to take my arm, when she saw Mrs Sen coming down the staircase. She just had time to whisper:

"Come to the library tomorrow, before dawn."

Those were the last words that I heard on Maitreyi's lips. Her mother escorted her off and I went back to my room – shattered, distraught, incapable of thinking about what would happen.

I could not sleep. Seated in my large armchair, I smoked pipe after pipe, waiting for dawn. A clock chimed the hours into the night, each time reviving the hope that Maitreyi was about to arrive in my room. I could not believe I would never again see her here, at my side, ready to undress as soon as I had closed the shutters, ready to kiss me and to cry with joy. It was impossible that after just two or three weeks of love, Maitreyi was to be taken from me. Alone in the darkness, I visualized every detail of her naked body, saw her in each one of her lover's postures. I forgot the torments I had endured because of her, the agonising doubts, and I felt growing inside me a love without limits, a love that Maitreyi had never suspected. I waited for the dawn impatiently, so that I could tell her that one night of separation and a vague sense of danger had taught me real love, that it was only on that day – the day I might lose her forever – that I had understood how precious she was to me.

Alone in the night, I was on the verge of tears at the idea of losing Maitreyi. I was trembling, my mind was restless. I did not think I would be able to survive our separation. When I had been certain she belonged to me, when no one had stopped me from speaking to her, going to her, I had loved her – now, when difficulties and an unknown threat hung over us, the strength of my love was almost suffocating me. I was overwhelmed by a desire to see her, clasp her in my arms. I felt as if I were losing my mind.

Several times during the night I went to walk around the garden. A light was still shining in the engineer's room. Voices, sometimes broken by a plaintive moan, drifted down from above. Was it Maitreyi, Chabu, Khokha's sister? I could not tell. I was in extremes of anguish. I went back to my room, threw myself into my armchair and began speculating once more on what Maitreyi's words could have meant: "Chabu has told Mama everything." What had she said, in her madness? What had she seen and understood? Could she have seen her sister leaving their room at night to come to me?

Khokha told me later what had happened. Chabu's revelations had in fact been much more trivial. Mrs Sen had been washing Chabu's head and the child had cried incessantly; her mother had asked her why she was so sad. Chabu had replied that no one loved her, while everyone loved Maitreyi: everyone had come on her birthday and had given her presents. "Alain especially," she had added, "prefers Maitreyi."

"How do you know?" her mother had asked her.

"Alain kisses her and puts his hand on her chest. No one kisses me..."

Her tears and her sorrow had seemed so genuine that Mrs Sen questioned her closely. Chabu finally told her everything she had seen: at the lakes we laughed, kissed, hugged each other. (And I had thought that Chabu noticed nothing!)

Mrs Sen had called Maitreyi to her at once and asked her if Chabu had been telling the truth. And then she ordered the chauffeur to put the car in the garage and had taken her daughter up to the roof. There, threatening her violently, she had made her swear, by her ancestors and by the gods, that it was not true. Maitreyi denied everything. She acknowledged only that she had kissed me several times on the cheek, in play, and that I had kissed her on the forehead in the same spirit. Nothing else had occurred between us. On her knees, she had begged her mother not to say anything to the engineer: I should not have to suffer any penalty because I was not guilty of any crime. If they insisted, she would accept never to see me again and to be punished for the fault that she alone had committed. I found out later that she was hoping to win time and to run away with me. Above all, she feared her father: he would have been capable of shutting her up in her room or marrying her off within a few days, without giving her time to see me again or to plan our escape.

She had been shut in her mother's room. Mrs Sen had told the engineer everything and sat up late into the night with him, discussing what they should do to hide the scandal from the neighbours... Maitreyi's misdeeds would bring down a curse that might fall on the entire family, bringing them disaster and ignominy and a disgrace which would have ruined them all...

At four o'clock in the morning, I went to the library to wait for her. I stayed there, hidden behind the shelves, until daybreak. Maitreyi did not come. I thought she might be able to send a message through Khokha's sister or Lilu; they did not come either. At about seven o'clock, Mrs Sen came down to prepare the tea. With infinite caution, afraid of being seen, I went back to my room.

I waited to be called for breakfast. But no one came. And then the engineer appeared, his eyes hidden behind his dark glasses, his walk unsteady, his hands trembling.

"My dear Alain, I have decided to have that operation which the doctors have been recommending for so long..."

He seemed agitated but his voice had its usual tone of sincere friendliness.

"I will have to stay at the clinic for two or three months. I am thinking of sending the family to relatives at Midnapore. You also are rather tired, you would do well to go and relax in the mountains."

"When must I leave?" I asked, with a calmness that surprised me.

In truth, I no longer knew what I was feeling. I went through that day as though I were anaesthetized, performing every action like a robot or a sleepwalker.

"Today," the engineer replied. "I leave for the clinic immediately after lunch."

He looked at me through his tinted lenses. I found the courage to make some small resistance, even though I felt as if my veins had been drained of blood.

"Very well, but I do not know where to go, I will have to find accommodation, I will have to take all my belongings – "

I indicated my bed, my chest of drawers, my bookcase, my two trunks.

The engineer smiled amiably.

"An energetic lad like you will always fall on his feet. If you leave at once you will be able to find a room before lunch. Khokha will bring your belongings to you this afternoon in a van. You can stay with one of your friends until you leave for the mountains. When you come back, you can find more comfortable lodgings..."

He got up. I was shaking from head to foot. I made towards the chest to get my topee, ready to leave that very moment. However, Mrs Sen, who was waiting in the corridor and had heard everything, came into the room and said to me with a smile:

"You cannot leave without eating!"

"I cannot eat anything," I said, in a faint voice.

"It is I who is asking and you will eat: the tea is ready," she replied, in the same gentle tone.

"What is the good, now?"

I felt as if I was going to faint, at any moment. So, I was leaving! I would never see Maitreyi again! I did not even know what was happening to her...

The engineer left and I collapsed into sobs, pulling my hair and biting my knuckles like a madman. I threw myself into the chair, obliterated, almost suffocating from a pain for which I had no name. It was neither frustrated love nor sorrow but rather a feeling of total dissolution. I had suddenly woken up alone in a cemetery, with no one to hear my woes or comfort me. I had been broken into a thousand pieces, my body nothing but a gaping wound, my soul destroyed. I no longer had the will or the strength to shake off the torpor that had descended on me.

Lilu came into the room, in tears, and shoved a piece of paper into my hand.

"They will not let me see you. Do not waste your life. Do not let yourself drown. Go back across the world and show your purity to them all. Be a man. I will send a message to you soon. Maitreyi."

The handwriting was shaky; it had obviously been written in haste. There were ink stains on the paper. Suddenly, Mrs Sen came in, followed by a servant; I hid the note quickly.

"Please drink a cup of tea," she said, in a voice of great sweetness.

I thought I sensed a note of pity and almost of understanding in that voice. I remembered the kindness she had shown me. She had been very fond of me, called me her son – she who had so much wanted a son after her two daughters.

I almost threw myself at her feet, to ask her forgiveness, beg her to let me stay, but when I looked at her again she was standing by the doorway stiff, silent and immobile, a frozen, slightly mocking smile on her lips.

"Could I see the children before I go?" I asked her.

At that moment, Narendra Sen came in.

"Maitreyi is ill," he said, "she cannot come down from her room."

Then, addressing his wife:

"Have Chabu called."

Alone with me, the engineer handed me a sealed envelope.

"I ask you not to read this until you have left my house. If you want to thank me for the kindness that I have shown you here in India, do as I ask..."

He left, without giving me time to reply. Mechanically, I put the letter in my pocket.

When I saw Chabu, I lifted her into my arms and cradled her, tears pricking my eyelids.

"What have you done, Chabu? What have you done?" I asked her, pressing my face against her frail little body.

The poor child did not understand, but seeing that I was crying, began crying herself and kissing me. Hardly conscious of what I was doing, I rocked her against me, incapable of saying anything other than "What have you done, Chabu? What have you done?"

Suddenly, she seemed to find her reason and asked, "But

what could I have known? Why are you crying, Alain, why are you crying?"

I put her down and wiped my face. Mrs Sen and her husband stayed by the door, motionless, as though turned to stone. They seemed to be saying "Come, it is time! Leave!"

I kissed the child once more on her cheeks and, finding some spirit, took leave of my hosts.

"Goodbye, Alain," said the engineer in English, holding out his hand.

I pretended I had not seen it and began walking down the corridor. Chabu ran after me, sobbing, "Where are you going, Alain?" and then, to her mother, "Where is he going?"

"Alain is ill, he is going to get better," Mrs Sen replied, in a low voice, holding her back.

I climbed down the veranda steps and looked up towards the wisteria balcony. I caught sight of Maitreyi. She cried out my name. A brief, terrified cry. And then I saw her fall to the floor. Without thinking, instinctively, I started running up to her. The engineer blocked my way.

"Have you forgotten something?"

"No, nothing."

I left then, jumping into the first taxi that passed, giving Harold's address. I wanted to look back once more at the house but my eyes were full of tears; the car turned a corner and it had disappeared from view.

By the time I had returned to my senses a little, the car was entering Park Street. I tore open the envelope and read Sen's letter, a knot of pain in my chest. He had written in English, without any opening salutation and in the corner of the sheet he had written and underlined, "Strictly Confidential."

"You are a stranger. I do not know you. If you are capable of regarding anything as sacred, I ask you not to enter my house again, not to attempt to see or write to any member of my family. If you want to see me, you can do so at the office. If you ever want to write to me, write only as one stranger to

another or as an employee to his superior. I ask you not to
mention this note to anyone and to destroy it when you have
read it. The reasons for my actions will be obvious to you if the
slightest trace of sanity remains in you. You are surely aware of
your own ingratitude and the wrong that you have perpetrated
against me!

NARENDRA SEN

P.S. I ask you not to cause trouble by attempting to exonerate
yourself: you will only be adding new lies to those which your
depraved character has already told."

XIII

Harold was out, but his landlady let me into his room. I threw myself on to the bed and lay in the cool of the fan. Poor Mrs Ribeiro, overcome with embarrassment, was at a loss for words.

"Nothing drastic has happened," I reassured her. "My boss, Mr Sen, is having his operation today and I am worried about him."

I did not want to tell this woman or Harold anything, or to give myself away. Their commiserations would have unnerved me completely. Harold would have been falling over himself to tell all to his Anglo-Indian "friends", the girls would have tried to console me with their trite sentimental formulas, encouraging me to drink, to go out – and I could not bear any consolation, even of the brutal variety. I felt as though I did not have the right to speak Maitreyi's name to those people. I was shell-shocked, absorbed entirely in my pain, my mind could rest on nothing, I tried only to grasp – clearly and lucidly – the idea that Maitreyi and I had been separated. Impossible. I shook with horror every time that last image appeared in front of me: her body stretched out on the balcony. I forced the vision to disappear and fixed my mind on more comforting scenes: the little wreath of jasmine, the library, Chandernagor... I became a little calmer, but at once the film began again, speeded up and replayed the last scenes: Mrs Sen, at table, looking at me maliciously, Mr Sen saying "If you want to thank me for all the kindness I have shown you...", and again the sharp stabbing pain of separation coursed through me. I closed my eyes and breathed deeply, trying to ward off the remorseless onslaught of my thoughts.

After an hour, Mrs Ribeiro came back and asked me what I wanted to drink: tea, whisky or beer? I refused everything, with a gesture so weary that the old lady approached the bed, seriously worried.

"But you are ill, Alain!"

"I don't know what's wrong. I have been overworking for the last few months. I have not had a holiday this summer and Mr Sen's troubles have affected me deeply. I want to leave Calcutta for a while. Do you still have a vacant room, Mrs Ribeiro?"

At the words "vacant room", Mrs Ribeiro was overcome with joy and she made me get up at once to inspect it. She asked me why I had not stayed at Bhowanipore, but seeing her curiosity was unwelcome, changed the subject. She was worried that I was feverish and advised me to leave immediately for the mountains, to spend several weeks in Darjeeling for example, or in Shillong, or else by the sea, at Gopalpur where Father Justus had gone to cure his nervous exhaustion: the air was marvellous and the hotels almost empty. I listened to her talking and nodded, so that I would not have to speak, to respond, to think. She brought in a copy of *The Statesman* from the hall and looked through it for addresses of boarding-houses, telling me as she did so what person had stayed at each place and with what ailment. I felt as though I were living in a dream. My presence here seemed hardly possible, the apparent reality of my body stretched out on the bed, the cigarettes I was smoking, seemed to me absurd – because I was going to die, because I had to die: Maitreyi had been torn away from me. Without formulating the question in words but somehow feeling it inside myself, I wondered how such a thing could have happened. How, an hour after leaving Bhowanipore, could I be here listening to the burblings of this old lady, who had no idea of my utter desolation? It all seemed inconceivable, impossible and I felt I would go mad if I stayed in such surroundings for much longer, if I did not go and bury myself somewhere, anywhere, alone – to forget, to forget myself. To leave seemed my only chance of salvation, at least for a while. I decided to go the next day.

"Please telephone Mr Sen, on South 1144," I asked Mrs Ribeiro, "and ask for my things to be brought here."

At any other time, Mrs Ribeiro would have considered it an affront to her dignity to have to telephone a 'negro' but on this occasion she was so happy to do so that she spoke – probably to Mantu – with extreme politeness, falling over herself with thanks.

"I'll go and prepare your room," she said to me.

I was happy to see her go. I was now free to sigh and weep as much as I wanted. The idea suddenly came to me that I must have aged overnight and that my hair must be white. I ran to a mirror; I hardly recognized myself. My face was haggard, thin, pale, my eyebrows dishevelled and sparse. A wrinkle had appeared at the corner of my lips, giving me a severe, hard expression that astounded me since I had in fact lost all masculine decisiveness and power of action. I have given no credence to physiognomy since then. A face does not change in rhythm with the experiences that the mind undergoes; only the eyes, perhaps, reveal the truth of a man.

Overcome, I went back to my bed and lit another cigarette. The door opened. It was Harold, who had been told of my arrival by Mrs Ribeiro. He gave a cry of delight at seeing me. He tried to make me talk, but I pretended to have a headache and told him in a few words why I was there. He had refreshments brought up, assuring me that whisky was the cure for all fever and pain. I drank a glass, but the first waves of intoxication only made my unhappiness more acute. I was on the verge of screaming.

When I saw Khokha, I could have hugged him. His presence brought back all my love, all India to me. He was dressed in a grubby dhoti and his gnarled feet were bare. The household and the neighbours looked at him with contempt and disgust but he, feeling he was in my home, went to and fro with an air of great disdain, giving offhand orders to the porters who were emptying the van. I waited impatiently for him to tell me what was happening at Bhowanipore. I paid the men and brought him into my room. I asked Mrs Ribeiro for tea and opened a packet of cigarettes. Harold was fuming: he wanted to speak to me alone. But perhaps he guessed that my abrupt departure from Narendra Sen's was not as innocuous as I had given him to understand. He dared not come into the room to disturb us. Khokha had brought me a copy of *Uddhita*, on which Maitreyi had written her final words "To my love, to my love, Maitreyi, Maitreyi."

"Is that all?" I asked sadly.

Khokha told me to look at the back of the book. She had written: "Adieu, my darling, I have said nothing that incriminates you, only that you kissed me on the forehead. I had to admit it, it was our mother and she knew. Alain, my friend, my love, adieu! Maitreyi."

I contemplated the message dumbly. Khokha smoked, also silent and then suddenly he said, as if speaking his thoughts aloud:

"And then they found out. You were too careless. Everyone saw you when you were kissing on the armchair. It was fatal. The chauffeur told Mantu and Lilu. No one was brave enough to warn you..."

I wondered whether Khokha knew more than the others; suddenly I realized it no longer mattered.

"Chabu has returned to her senses. When she saw Maitreyi faint, it was as if she suddenly woke up. She asked everyone where you were – she kept pulling Mrs Sen's sari and asking. I told her that I was coming to see you and she gave me this note."

On a sheet of paper torn from a school exercise book, Chabu had written in her best handwriting: "Dear Alain, will you be able to forgive me one day? I do not know why I spoke. I did not think I was doing any harm because you were not doing any harm by loving each other. Maitreyi is suffering terribly. Can you do something so that she does not suffer any more? What has happened to your love now? I would like to die."

"She was crying when she wrote that and she told me to be certain that I gave it to you. She wants you to telephone her. She is not mad any more, she doesn't act mad. The poor thing..."

He stopped for a moment and then suddenly sighed.

"What is the matter, Khokha?" I asked.

"What is the good of telling you what the matter is, when I can see you are suffering just as much as me!"

He had declaimed this in a theatrical tone, putting on a pained, tragic face. All at once, he seemed to me a total stranger. He must have seen my indifference and changed the subject.

"When I started to take your things, Maitreyi came down to kiss them. She was shouting. They had to drag her back. Mr Sen, the brute, hit her in the face until she bled... she fainted in her room."

Tears came to my eyes as I listened to him, but my sense of pain was no greater than it had been before. What more could they do to us than to separate us? If I were beaten, slapped, would my suffering be any greater? I visualized Maitreyi, her face bloodied; yet what gripped my heart was not her wounds but the knowledge that she was far from me, that her being itself was far from me.

"They shut her in her room, practically naked, to stop her coming down to yours. They took away all the books you had given her. When she fainted, they splashed her with water but when she came round she shouted 'I love him, I love him', and they beat her again. From downstairs, I could only hear her screaming, but my sister told me that she also shouted 'He is not guilty! What do you have against him? What?'"

I did not understand Maitreyi's concern for me. Her parents

had not done anything to me as yet. It would have been better if Mr Sen had had courage enough to slap me, for example. Why had he held out his hand, like a coward, saying "Goodbye, Alain"?

"Maitreyi had the time to whisper to me, 'I will telephone him tomorrow', before being taken to her room. But she won't be able to. Mr Sen is keeping her locked up. I heard him talking to 'Mama' about a quick marriage..."

That news froze me with horror. Khokha saw my reaction and went on with renewed enthusiasm:

"Yes, they want to marry her to a teacher from Hooghly, as soon as they get back from Midnapore. You know they are leaving for Midnapore?"

"I know."

"They are brutes. They are all brutes. Don't you hate them?"

"Why should I hate them? It is I who have done them wrong. What have they done? The only wrong they did was in bringing me to the house."

"They wanted to adopt you..."

I smiled. How vain and useless it all seemed! To dream of what might have been if I had been different, to dream of my eventual happiness – what idiocy! I was alone, all alone – that was my pain, my reality, my present. I could not conceive of it any other way.

Khokha saw I was crying and sighed.

"My mother is very ill and I have no money to give her. I was thinking of borrowing something from you, while waiting for my money from the Bengal Film Company..."

"How much do you want?"

He was silent. I did not dare look him in the eyes. His lies were painful to me. I knew that his mother was well and that one of his brothers-in-law, a shop-keeper in Kalighat, looked after her.

"Will thirty rupees be enough?"

Without waiting for a reply, I made out the cheque and gave it to him.

He thanked me, embarrassed and began speaking to me about Maitreyi again. In a weak voice I asked him to leave.

"Khokha, I am tired, I have a headache."

In the evening the girls came to see me, having been alerted by Harold. They installed the gramophone in the hall and ordered whisky and orangeade. To cheer me up, they feigned an atmosphere of great hilarity. Harold had told them I was suffering from nervous depression due to overwork. Before leaving Calcutta, I had to "enjoy myself", to forget everything.

"So, Alain," said Gertie, "why are you sitting there all sulky, my lad? Can't you see your girlfriend is here?"

She sat on my lap; that contact sent such a shiver of revulsion through me that I begged her to leave me alone.

"I am tired and I don't feel well."

"You are not in love, by any chance?" she said, winking at the others maliciously. "Might some Indian have bewitched you? Do you know what Indian women wash with? Cow dung. I swear it – every time they commit a sin they go to the Ganges and wash with cow dung..."

They all screamed with laughter. Mrs Ribeiro, who was tidying my room next door, came in.

"Why don't you leave the poor boy alone! Come, Alain, drink a glass of whisky. You will see how everything gets better in time. An operation on the eyes is not so serious..."

"Do you really believe, Mrs Ribeiro, that Alain is crying because of Mr Sen's operation?" said Gertie, mockingly. "It's because of something much more serious. His fancy-girl has run off with a gypsy..."

"Shut up!" I shouted, filled with sudden rage, getting up from my chair.

"Would you kindly speak politely to me. You're not with your Bhowanipore negroes now!"

"Gertie!" Clara reproached her, taking her arm. "Leave him alone, the poor boy..."

"You have coddled him too much, all of you, with your 'poor boy' this, 'poor boy' that. He's crying like a woman. Let him go and be comforted by his dirty Bengal women! What right does he have to insult me – me, a Christian?"

"But he is Christian too!"

"You think he is still Christian?" said Gertie, bursting into laughter. "What do you think, Harold? Do you remember when he spoke to you about Hinduism and cows and insulted Our Lord? And now it's he who tells me to shut up!"

Harold did not know where to put himself. Mrs Ribeiro gave way to panic.

"Come along, calm down, calm down!" she cried.

"I'm leaving," I said to them all, getting up.

Gertie looked at me sulkily.

"He's going to pray at his temple..."

I spent a feverish night. I could not sleep and I went out to wander through the streets, only half conscious, smoking end-less cigarettes. I sought out native areas where the swarming crowds of people, the noise, the shouts in dialect, brought back to me our nocturnal walks around the town. When I finally returned to the house, the torment, which I had hoped to stifle with fatigue, descended on me once more; this time I was utterly powerless against it. I bit my pillow, hit myself in a vain attempt to stop my cries, repeating "Maitreyi, Maitreyi, Maitreyi," until the name had no more power of association and I fell silent, my face buried in the pillow, not knowing any longer what had happened, what it was that had broken inside me. My mind jumped from image to image, without connec-tion. I saw Tamluk, Sadyia, innumerable other places that I had known, but without understanding any of it. I had only one fear: thoughts of anything that reminded me of Maitreyi on the day of our separation, the voice of Mr Sen saying "Goodbye,

Alain," or Mrs Sen's expression as she insisted, "Have some tea!" Whenever such visions assailed me, I fought them off with all my strength.

Harold was snoring in the room next door. Throughout the night, I heard the clock of the Protestant church chime the hours. I abandoned myself to my thoughts. I would drown myself in the Ganges and Mr Sen would realize how much I had loved his daughter; the next day, the papers would report the motiveless suicide of a young European, discovered at the outskirts of the town by boatmen returning in the evening. Maitreyi would faint at the news. Mrs Sen would feel remorse. She would understand then that I had loved Maitreyi sincerely, with all my soul.

Thoughts of my death became my sole consolation. I dwelt voluptuously on every detail, on every act that would have to be performed. I saw myself writing a final letter to Mr Sen, walking towards the bridge, shedding – softly, almost imperceptibly – a few tears. And then I would lean against the safety barrier, watching the yellowish, muddy water as it flowed past – a little dizziness and then I would be ready... The film over, I played it again, and again, until I dozed off at dawn.

Harold woke me: someone was on the telephone for me. I tore down the hall like a lunatic, in my pyjamas. I recognized Maitreyi's voice at once. Like a man dying of thirst who is given fresh water, I drank in her every word. I was afraid of replying, of being overheard by Harold or another lodger. I caught only snatches of what she was saying. She was speaking quietly – doubtless so as not to wake her family – and she continually broke into sobs. Her voice sounded as if it came from the depths of a cavern or a locked cell – it was so broken, so different from its old sweetness.

"Alain! Do you recognize me? It's me, it's really me! I will not change, Alain, no matter what happens... Be a man, continue to work. Do not despair. I cannot take any more, Alain. Forgive me. I cannot take any more. I wanted to say to you..."

Suddenly, she broke off. Someone, probably Mrs Sen, had caught her. I cried vainly, "Hello, hello," – no one was there. I went back to my room, utterly broken. I wanted to escape, there and then. The sight of my few possessions tortured me, especially the straw armchair on which Maitreyi had so often sat. Each one of those wretched objects reminded me of a scene, a word. I was incapable of freeing myself from these obsessional thoughts, of putting an end to this emotional delirium which had transformed me, in one day, from man into ghost.

"How is the engineer? Has he had the operation?" asked Harold.

"Not yet," I replied, at random. "Today, perhaps."

"The poor man."

I collapsed on to my bed and lit another cigarette. I felt as if my body had become paralysed, apart from my hands which shook ceaselessly. My face had frozen, was without expression. I stayed there, underneath the fan, not knowing what to do, incapable of foreseeing my future.

Around ten o'clock, a boy on a bicycle stopped outside the house. He had a message for me. No reply was expected.

It was a letter from Narendra Sen.

"Sir,

I have today been given to understand that you have neither respect nor honour. I thought you were simply mad but I see now that you are like a snake in the grass whose head must be cut off to ensure that he will not turn against us and bite us. Not even twenty-four hours have elapsed since you gave me your word of honour that you would not try to communicate with any member of my family. You have broken your word like a coward and you have caused suffering to a poor child upon whom, unfortunately, you have exercised some influence. If you attempt another such communication, I will do my utmost to have you repatriated. I thought you would have the good sense to leave our town. I have telephoned the office to order your dismissal, as from today. All that remains for you to do is to collect your wages and to leave immediately. There must be a limit to your ingratitude.

NARENDRA SEN"

When I had read the letter, I fell back on the bed, appalled. Not because of my dismissal: I had decided myself to leave the job. I could never see Sen again, after having heard Khokha's account of what he had done to his daughter. But I knew that Maitreyi would continue to commit such follies and to bear the increasingly horrific consequences. I suffered ten times more than she at the idea of the punishments she would suffer. I knew that I could give her no help and the knowledge of my powerlessness and my separation from her tortured me.

I put the letter back in the envelope and went out, taking only my topee.

"Will you have lunch here, Alain?" asked Mrs Ribeiro. "I have cooked your favourite things. Harold told me what they were, you see. Now, don't worry yourself any more..."

I smiled and closed the door, numb. The idea came to me that I should withdraw some money from the bank – in case I needed to leave Calcutta in a hurry, although I had no idea where I would go. I would not leave on Sen's orders. His threats left me unmoved. I would go because I knew that only my departure could really help Maitreyi: she would be able to forget me... I realized that I was reasoning like a child. Even though it was a good distance, I walked to the bank in Clive Street.

I arranged the bank notes into a tidy wad, put them in my wallet and distributed the coins to my pockets. And then I went to the station. As I crossed the Howrah bridge I leaned over to look at the Ganges, dirty and crowded with small boats. The idea of killing myself suddenly seemed cowardly and ridiculous. At the station buffet, I drank a glass of lemonade. It was mid-day. I left the station and turned right into the ring road which leads to the outlying villages, passing through Belur. As soon as I had set off down the well-shaded street I felt stronger, calmer and I began to walk with energy and determination. I walked without stopping, not smoking, taking large strides – with what must have looked a lively, decided air. The taxis which ferry people between the station and Hooghly passed me in both directions; almost all of them stopped. The drivers were amazed to see a European walking on the main road, outside the town. I stopped only once, at a wretched little hut, where an old woman was selling lemonade, bread and chillis. I drank a glass of the cool liquid. I spoke to the old woman in Bengali, rather than Hindustani as I should have done. That conversation heartened me. The words I spoke – in Maitreyi's language – had all the softness of balm.

I arrived at Belur-Math at half past two. It had rained for the last two miles of my journey, I was soaked to the skin and my clothes were splashed with mud. I met Swami Madhvananda, a monk whom I knew from my visits to Belur in the engineer's car; my appearance and my wild expression obviously alarmed him. I went to the bank of the Ganges to dry out. Stretched out on the grass, the sun on my face, I conjured up in my mind all the times I had walked here at Maitreyi's side, free of care.

I could not stand it any longer. Unable to shed any more tears, I took my notebook from my pocket and began writing. Today I re-read those lines that seemed at the time to have been written with the very blood from my veins; they seem to me now cold and banal. For example: "Everything is over! Why? An immense emptiness inside. Nothing has meaning any more. Hearing a Bengali chant, up there in the *math*, makes me want to cry. Maitreyi, Maitreyi, Maitreyi. Never to see her again..." How incapable we are of capturing the substance of vivid joy or pain at the moment of its experience. I believe that hindsight is necessary, that only memory can truly resuscitate emotion. A diary is too dry, too trivial.

The swami tried to find out what had happened to me. When I told him that I had walked from Calcutta – and without eating because I could not eat – he took fright and asked me to go back

at once or I would fall ill, catch malaria (he knew of my attack
last year) or some other misfortune would befall me... His tone
was authoritarian. Doubtless he despised me because I had let
myself be overcome with passion and sadness. These Hindu
monks cannot comfort anyone: a soul bound by suffering seems
unworthy to them of all pity. Their atrocious ideal of detach-
ment puts them in another world to that inhabited by the poor
human being, who suffers, who struggles in his experience of
life. Those people live too divinely to descend from their state
of perfect, supreme serenity. I had not, in any case, come to
Belur-Math for sympathy. I had come simply because I hoped
that I would rediscover Maitreyi as she existed in my memory,
the real Maitreyi, my Maitreyi. The swami's words did not
offend me. They simply made me feel still more alone. I left,
thanking him for the fruits and the gentle words that he had
none the less asked a fellow monk to speak to me.

I did not turn back but continued on the same road, towards
Ranaghat. I arrived at Rally at sunset. I looked for the Ganges,
and then, seated on a rock, smoking peacefully, contemplated it
for a long time. I sat marvelling at the vast stretch of water,
flowing silently back to Calcutta. Some children approached
and surrounded me. At first they squealed, in garbled English,
"White monkey!" Then, seeing that I did not get angry but
only looked at them, tears in my eyes, they came closer and
stood there awkwardly until I spoke to them in Bengali and
distributed some coins. They escorted me in procession to the
other end of the village.

The evening was cool and still after the rains, inviting one to
walk. Soon I was alone again on the main road. Cars occasionally sped past me, their headlights full on, on their way to
Calcutta. At times I met a man or a couple of men, hurry-
ing... How early people went to bed in India! I thought of
Bhowanipore and a warm tide of emotion rose in my throat. I
pressed on. I stopped at a roadside shop to buy "Scissor"
cigarettes, the only brand they sold. An acetylene lamp burned

in the room and several passers-by were relaxing around it, placidly taking large puffs on the hookah. They all turned to stare at me, astounded; one man even came out on to the road to watch me walk off into the darkness.

I do not know for how long I walked or what villages I crossed. I felt neither tiredness nor pain. That walk through the blackness had begun to enchant me. It stifled my thoughts and induced in me a kind of self-satisfied contentment. I believed I was accomplishing that feat of endurance through overwhelming suffering and for love of Maitreyi.

By the roadside, several feet from the ditch, I saw a covered fountain and I stopped to rest. Without realising, I drifted off to sleep, my head resting against my topee, stretched out on the bare stones. My dreams, haunted once again by Maitreyi's image, made me wake with a start several times and I trembled with fear, loneliness and cold. Some men arrived at the fountain and their noise awoke me. They looked at me, incredulous. None of them dared speak to me. My clothes were muddy, my canvas shoes torn to shreds but they could see I was still a sahib – a white sahib, at that.

I splashed my face with water and began walking again, more quickly this time. I was worried: there would be traffic on the road at daybreak. I walked, keeping my head down and did not stop until, through the palm-trees, I caught sight of the Ganges. That view of the river was strangely comforting: I knew that it led to the town where I myself was going, the town where Maitreyi was. The reasons for my unhappiness were no longer clear to me. I barely thought about what Harold or Mrs Ribeiro would say on my return. A single idea cheered me: perhaps Khokha would come to see me. When he found out that I had disappeared the day before and had not returned, he would tell the engineer. I would have liked Sen to think that I had died and to have to reflect on his behaviour towards me.

I ate in a roadside inn outside Ranaghat: curried rice and boiled fish. I ate with my hand, in the Indian fashion, much to the surprise and delight of the other diners, who had already heard me speak in proficient Bengali; my appearance must, however, have perplexed them. I was sure that my face was drawn, unshaven and my hair unkempt. My clothes were dirty and my hands black. I set off again; as I walked, I began to forget everything, even myself, and that realisation gave me a new, vigorous appetite for the road. I walked until sundown, without passing any villages, meeting only bullock carts or an occasional ancient, creaking lorry. The day was scorchingly dry and I stopped at every fountain to drink and to soak my face. When the stars came out, I stretched out beside a giant mango-tree that stood alone at the edge of a deserted pond. The mosquitoes tormented me long into the night but my exhaustion finally took over and I fell asleep; I did not wake until late into the morning, my limbs cramped, almost totally numb... I must have had some terrible nightmare: I was sweating with fear and still shaking. I forced myself up and almost ran off down the road.

I walked all day, in that torrid heat. I remember nothing of it, except that I asked the driver of a bullock cart, dream-like, where I was and how I could get to a station. He directed me to a stop in the outskirts of Burdwan. I arrived late at night. The first train for Calcutta did not pass until dawn and did not stop. An omnibus left for Burdwan at around midnight. I took a third class ticket: I did not have the courage to enter a second or first class compartment.

At Burdwan, I was disturbed by the violently lit station. I felt like a sick man who had been brutally woken and shoved into the thick of a crowd. Stunned, helpless, I did not know which counter I should go to for a third class ticket; I was ashamed of standing among the old women and the scarecrows who were milling around it. Ashamed not for myself but on behalf of the few Anglo-Indians and Englishmen, also waiting for the fast train from Lucknow, who cast suspicious glances at my clothes.

Mechanically, I gulped down glass after glass of tea at the buffet, trying to piece together the last few days. There were

large chunks missing and those gaps in my memory worried me
obsessively. Had I gone mad? I resolved not to think any more.
Everything passes in time, everything passes, I told myself and
that leitmotif, which comforted me for the first time on that
day, has comforted me ever since.

At Howrah station, a new emotion. I was frightened that I
would meet someone from Bhowanipore. But then I remembered that the Sen family must have left for Midnapore and
that thought, which had at first tormented me because it meant
that Maitreyi had been taken even further from me, brought
now a certain relief. There was no risk of my running into
Narendra Sen in the town.

The taxi deposited me at the boarding house at the very
moment the Park Street police were beginning their investiga-
tion into my disappearance. When she saw me get out of the
car, my topee misshapen, my chin covered with a four-day
beard and my clothes filthy, Mrs Ribeiro almost fainted.

"Where have you been? My God, where have you been?
South 1144 has not stopped telephoning and that boy,
Khokha, has come asking after you all the time. My God, my
God!"

I let her run on and went to wash. A bath! At that moment, it
was all I wanted. Harold telephoned from his office to know if
there was any news of me; Mrs Ribeiro told him I had returned
and in what a state! He jumped into a taxi as fast as he could to
come and see me.

"So, old chap! So, old chap!" he repeated, overcome, grip-
ping my hand.

His effusiveness warmed me. I tapped him on the shoulder to
help him come to himself.

"It's nothing, old man! I'll be all right. But what's been
happening? Where have you been?"

"I went for a walk. Nothing serious, just a walk."

I smiled at him.

"And you? How are you?"

"Yesterday the girls came over in quite a state. We were going to organize something in China Town to celebrate your liberation from the clutches of the idolaters...So, old chap! What got into you? Your negro came looking for you. I think he's rather angry. He got on my nerves, I threw him out. 'Alain has become a Christian again,' I told him."

After dinner, Khokha telephoned me, from a bookshop in the Ashntosh Mukherjee Road, where he has friends. Speaking hurriedly, he told me that serious events had occurred; he absolutely had to see me. I told him to take a taxi and waited for him on the veranda.

"So where did you go?" he asked as soon as he saw me.

"I'll tell you later," I told him abruptly. "Tell me what has happened first."

Much, it seemed, had happened. They had tried to marry Maitreyi off but she had declared she would tell her husband, on her wedding night, that she had slept with me. The whole family would have been compromised, she would have been thrown out in disgrace and the entire town would know of her shame. The engineer had struck her full in the face and knocked her to the ground, bleeding. He had then had an attack and had been taken to hospital. He had gone blind. If he were well enough, they would operate in a day or two, but he was so agitated that the doctors were worried. As for Maitreyi, she had been locked in her room. Mrs Sen had called the chauffeur and ordered him to beat her daughter, in front of her, with a birch rod. He had beaten her until she lost consciousness. Mrs Sen had also asked Khokha to beat her but he had refused, had run off. Chabu had tried to kill herself by swallowing creosote. She was now in hospital, with her father.

Khokha gave me an envelope from Maitreyi. Inside was a little sprig of flowering oleander, which she had just had time to put in. On a sheet of paper she had written in pencil: "Alain, here is my last present..." She had asked me not to leave for five days. She knew nothing of my escapade (which was as well, she would have thought I had killed myself and who knows what folly she might have committed...)

I listened to Khokha as though in a dream, trying to feel the impact of this news and its possible consequences. But I could grasp nothing except the fact that Maitreyi was suffering even more and that she was imprisoned. Khokha asked me to write a few lines for her but, remembering my promise to Narendra Sen, I refused.

"What is the good?" I asked sadly. "What good, now? She should forget me! She must forget me, for four or five years, until she can be mine again..."

I suddenly realized that I was raving. I began to cry like an idiot; I felt the room spinning around me. I shouted:

"If only I could love her! If only I could! But I do not love her!"

Khokha looked at me, sniggering.

"I want to love her, I want to be capable of loving her!"

Mrs Ribeiro ran into the room, aghast, and asked me what was wrong. I was crying.

"I want to love Maitreyi! So why can I not love her? What have I done to them? What have they got against me? What do you all have against me?..."

The next thing I remember was a telephone call from Maitreyi one morning:

"Adieu, Alain, adieu my darling. We will meet each other in the next life, my darling. Will you recognize me then? Will you wait for me? Wait for me, Alain, do not forget me. I will wait for you. No one else will touch me."

I could say nothing except "Maitreyi, Maitreyi, Maitreyi..."

I left Calcutta on the seventh day after our separation; the previous two nights I had spent opposite their house, watching for a light in Maitreyi's room. The window remained dark the whole time.

The day I left, Chabu died.

XIV

The months I spent in the heart of the Himalayas, in a bungalow between Almora and Ranikhet, were months of sadness and tranquillity.

I arrived after having wandered from Delhi to Simla to Naini Tal, where there were too many people, especially whites. I was afraid of meeting people: I did not want to have to waste my time responding to their greetings, exchanging small talk with them. They prevented me from being alone; solitude was my rock of comfort, my sustenance.

Few people can have known an isolation as bitter and as desperate as mine. From October to February, I saw only one man here: the caretaker of my bungalow. I spoke to him, once or twice a day, when he brought me something to eat or refilled my pitcher of water. I spent all my time among the trees. The surroundings of Almora possess the most magnificent pine woods of the Himalayas. I explored the length and breadth of them, incessantly replaying the same interior film of my love, imagining all sorts of scenes, each more fantastic than the last. The climax was always the same – Maitreyi and I living happily ever after, in a still inviolate solitude, in the dead town of Fetehpur-Sikri or in an abandoned hut in the middle of the jungle.

I spent entire days watching the unfolding of this phantasmagoria, which had only one theme – our isolation from the rest of the world. Memories, long since forgotten, surged up in my mind and my imagination completed, deepened, connected them to each other. Details to which I had hitherto given no

importance now occupied the whole of my mental world.
Everywhere I went – under the pines and the chestnut-trees,
between the rocks and on the roads – I met Maitreyi. I lived in
the solace of this private tale so intensely that every call from
the outside world terrified me, made me almost physically ill. I
knew that, below in Bhowanipore, Maitreyi was thinking of me,
of the life we had lived together, just as intensely and that
communion of minds linked us, united us forever, even in
the face of separation and of death.

When it was full moon, I went down through the woods to
the torrent and there I would sit on a rock, watching the water,
shouting with all my strength: "Maitreyi, Maitreyi," until
exhaustion overcame me and my voice had become so weak
that it was no more than an inaudible whisper. I returned to the
bungalow by the same route, my soul indescribably healed. I
believed that Maitreyi had heard my call, that the water and the
wind had carried my words to her ears.

I do not know if the life I led during those months of complete solitude could be called a real existence, but it was the only
way that I could survive my ordeal. The energetic, optimistic
man that I had been existed no more. The youth, certain of
what he wanted and what he could achieve, the European
dedicated to science, with his pioneer spirit, who had arrived
in India believing he was bringing civilization with him, had
long since died. All that seemed useless now, illusory and
useless. All of it, apart from those few months of my love and
of my unhappiness. I suffered not simply because I had lost
Maitreyi but because I had wronged my benefactor, my incomparable 'Mama' and little Chabu – whose death, without any
doubt, I had caused. So much remorse almost suffocated me. I
had to anaesthetize it with the drug of a dream that grew ever
more powerful, which refused to recognize death, sin or
separation.

I re-read my diary continually, but never had the courage to
go as far as September 18th. It was, in any case, as though that

day had been eradicated from my mind. In a large envelope, I had sealed the few notes from Maitreyi, the engineer's letters, Chabu's letter, the sprig of oleander, a hairpin, several rough scribblings of Maitreyi's, mostly written at the time of our French lessons – the relics of the great passionate episode of my youth. (A few days ago, as I was writing these last chapters, I re-opened the envelope. What a depressing commentary I could write on those mementos and those memories...) I mostly read the earliest entries of my diary, laughing at my own candour and my emotional vanity, which had fooled me for so long.

I did not write to anyone – apart from a letter to my bank and a telegram informing Harold that I was still alive – and I received none. Once or twice a month the warden of the bungalow went to Naini Tal to buy provisions which he could not get in the villages of the valley.

Around Christmas time, I had a surprise which showed me how much I was still attached to the past and how dangerous it would have been for me to return to Calcutta. Khokha had learnt of my stay in the mountains from my bank and he had written to me via the poste restante at Naini Tal. When I read my name on the envelope that the warden had brought me, I could hardly believe it was truly meant for me. It was as though that Alain had ceased to exist long ago, had been left far away.

I bolted my door and read the message, trembling with emotion, as if I had suddenly found myself in the presence of Mr or Mrs Sen, or Maitreyi. Khokha wrote that the family had spent a month at Midnapore, from where Maitreyi herself had sent me a few lines, scribbled in haste on scraps of newspaper, bits of railway posters. She had added several simple field flowers, probably picked during her guarded walks to the edge of the village. She had suffered too much to retain a real, human, flesh-and-blood image of me. She had created another Alain and ascribed to him a whole glorious and untouchable

mythology. I had become for her a legendary figure which she
continually embroidered, placing me ever higher, ever further
from her, in unreality.

She wrote: "How could I lose you when you are my sun,
when your rays warm me on this country road? How could I
forget the sun?" On another fragment of paper she called me
'air' and 'flowers'. She added "Is it not you that I kiss when I
kiss this bunch of flowers which I clasp to my chest?" and "At
night you come to me as I used to come to you in our chamber
of love at Bhowanipore. But I came as a woman because you had
made me a woman. You come to me now like a god made of gold
and precious stones and I prostrate myself before you in wor-
ship because you are much more than my love, you are my sun,
my life!"

That escape into mythology pained me; it was extremely
strange to see myself increasingly idealized, transformed from
man into god, from lover into sun. I too had discovered the
realm of dreams but in my dreams it was always the same
Maitreyi of Bhowanipore that I met, that I clasped in my arms
with the same male hunger. My dream, fantastic as it was,
prolonged the life we had led together and the passion we
had known, taking both to a perfect completion. Maitreyi's
mythologizing converted me into an image, an idea, and I no
longer recognized myself in her 'sun' and her 'flowers', as I
would have wished to remain in her memory: a man of flesh and
blood, with his flaws and his passion.

A little knot of pain gripped my heart: why was Maitreyi
distancing herself from me? Why did she ask me to forget her,
in order to meet with her again in some future life? What did I
care for that future life with all the gods that she had peopled it
with? I was hungry for the real, the immediate, the living. I was
tormented by earthly memories, the memories of all that had
been living and irreplaceable in Maitreyi's body and soul. It was
she I desired, body and soul, she who appeared so solidly in my
daily film of our love. I did not want her to disappear into

unreality, to become an idea, a myth; I did not want to console myself with an eternal, celestial paradise.

Khokha gave me other news: the operation had not been very successful and the engineer had obtained leave for another six months. Mrs Sen's hair had gone white and her face now resembled a saint's. Maitreyi had become painfully thin. She stubbornly refused every proposal of marriage. Since returning to Calcutta, she continually telephoned me at Royd Lane. She believed they were lying to her, that I was still in town but that I did not want to see her. Khokha had gone to the boarding house but Mrs Ribeiro had complained to him that she had no news of me – I had told her I was going away for two or three weeks and I had now been away for four months, without sending word, apart from my telegram to Harold. Mantu had been thrown out because he had been insolent to the engineer. The poor man had fallen on hard times: he had to repay debts he had taken on for his wedding and he lived apart from Lilu, in a student hostel; she had gone to stay with her parents. He ate nothing but bread soaked in tea, in order to pay off the money as soon as possible and rejoin Lilu...

Khokha ended his letter by asking me when I thought I would return. He begged me not to forget my career or spoil my youth simply because of a love affair. All men had to go through such experiences. They had to emerge from them stronger, more resistant, not hide themselves away in the bosom of a mountain. That is not a solution. "So when will you return?" he asked in conclusion.

I often asked myself the same question but it was difficult to resign myself to the idea of going back to Calcutta. In any case, I did not know what I would do there: I had no job, my office had given me no reference and I could never go and ask for one. My savings would allow me to live in solitude for another year. But afterwards? I would start again from scratch, I would go far away, to Java for example, and there I would have the courage to begin a new life... Such ideas seemed no more than idle fantasies. I could not seriously envisage leaving India or taking a new job. All activities, ambitions, goals, seemed nothing but hollow vanities: merely to think of them left me with a feeling of emptiness. Seated on the veranda of my bungalow, I contemplated the pine forests and lost myself in thought...what was better, richer in meaning, than that forest? No one asked it why it grew nor for what eyes it displayed its incomparable beauty. How good to be a tree trunk, floating lightly, peacefully, happily on the waters of the Ganges... To feel nothing, to remember nothing.... Would that not give meaning to life, to return to the state of a simple mineral, to be changed into rock crystal, for example? To be a crystal, to live in and to radiate light, like a crystal...

I had brought no books with me and I welcomed any thought that chanced to come into my mind, as long as it pleased or comforted me. In my unbroken silence, I encountered men whom I imagined were like me but more profound, more vigorous, less captive. In my freedom, I languished as no prisoner ever had between four walls. I felt myself bound on all sides... there were even forbidden zones in my mind – that, for example, of around September 18th.

At the beginning of February, a stranger – a woman – arrived at the bungalow in the middle of the night. She woke the warden to demand a room. However, she spoke such an unintelligible gabble that the good man came to ask me to help. I put on my fur-lined Himalayan cloak, which gave me the air of a mountain mongol, and came out. She was lying across a couch on the veranda. She seemed worn out. I could see only her blonde hair and her over-large hands which clutched the two sides of a thin trench-coat to her body. Her face lit up when she saw me. She told me, breathing heavily and trembling, that she had left a servant in the courtyard with her luggage, that they had come on foot from Ranikhet, often having lost their way and having had to cross the torrent to get to the bungalow. She hinted at some disagreeable incident that had forced her to leave Rani-khet after nightfall. Her name was Jenny Isaac, she came from Cape Town in South Africa and had been in India for several months. She was wandering across the Himalayas, looking for a monastery that would take her in. I had the instant impression of a cold and lucid fanatic, who had been brought to this pass by some disillusionment rather than a real thirst to discover the truth.

The warden lit the large lantern in the bungalow and I was better able to see her: she was quite young, with blue eyes and a round, expressionless face; her girlish voice contrasted with her powerful well-built body, her high waist, her strong arms and large breasts. She was strangely dressed in colonial travel-ling clothes that had been adapted for mountain hiking. She was frozen to the bone and the warden had to make large quantities of tea for her which she swallowed eagerly, talking continually, asking me questions, as though worried on my account. Her presence seemed to me importunate and I was reassured to learn that she would not stay more than two days at the most. She wanted to reach Badrinath, at least thirty days walk away, stopping at Mikhali. I smiled at such a plan: the ridges were completely frozen, the paths covered with snow – and she had mistaken the route. She needed to go through Hardwar. I advised her to go to Kotdwara, from where she could take a train to Hardwar. She asked me if I was going somewhere myself or if I planned to stay at the bungalow. Such lack of discretion shocked me. I replied curtly that I did not know, that I would stay for the moment because the place had few visitors and because the air of these pine forests suited me perfectly...

The next day, I left at daybreak as usual. I walked around the mountain, bathed under a rock, ate honey biscuits and did not come back until nightfall. The warden announced that the lady, the memsahib, was ill and wanted to see me. How the devil had he been able to understand Jenny Isaac's tiny smattering of Hindustani? I knocked at the door. A voice, distorted by fever, replied. A tide of irritation arose in me. It seemed I must always be at some patient's bedside...

She was in bed, with a temperature and shivering, but fairly strong. She asked me if I would write a list of common words in Hindustani and make her a cup of cocoa as the warden did not know how... She seemed hardly affected by the reality of her situation: she had fallen ill, alone, in the heart of the mountains, ignorant of the language and unable to count on any help. She told me she had been suffering from fever for two or three weeks, that she had lain dying in the house of a Bhutani near Almora but that she had never been in the least frightened. I asked her, at random, what had made her come to India. She reddened slightly and then blurted out:

"I want to find the Absolute!"

I almost burst out with an enormous roar with laughter. With a sense both of sadness and relief, I realized I had suddenly rediscovered my sense of humour. I had thought that neither emotion nor a sense of the ridiculous could ever touch me again, that I had become indifferent to subtleties and nuances – and yet the seriousness with which this woman had pronounced the word 'Absolute' had all at once reawakened a whole world of farce and nonsense, of pseudo-mysticism and high drama – a world which I had inhabited for such a long time.

With great difficulty, I managed to change the subject. I asked her what she thought about Gandhi and the nationalist movement – insidious questions which I always ask when I want to distance myself from someone. She went on to tell me that she was a British citizen but that she belonged to a family of Finnish Jews who had settled in South Africa at the end of the last century, that she had been unable to stand the hypocrisy of the whites and that she had come here, determined to forget everything, to enter an ashram to find truth, life, immortality.

Impassive, I listened as she regurgitated all the popular superstitions about a mystical, magical India, all the nonsense of
Ramacharaka's books, all the foolishness of the Indian
pseudo-culture, so fashionable in Anglo-Saxon countries. It
was obvious that she had been alone for a long time and that
she was burning to tell me 'everything', happy to have found a
man to listen to her, to 'understand' her. Her revelations poured
out: she had four sisters, was a cellist for the municipal orchestra
of Cape Town and had given concerts at Johannesburg. She
earned £40 sterling a month. She did not get on with her family
– bourgeoisie whose sole preoccupation was to marry her off...
She had left them to live in a farm on the outskirts of the city, to
which she drove back every night after the concert, in a little car
which she had bought with her savings.

She would have continued in this vein but I pretended I was
worried that it was too late for me to be in her bedroom. I asked
her if she needed anything else and left, squeezing her hand
very properly and wishing her a speedy recovery.

I reflected for a long time that night on the illusory nature of
that 'Absolute' which the poor musician was seeking. I felt
great pity for her. She had left her home, her freedom in a
civilized country – simply because she had come across the
books of that English trickster writing under the pseudonym
of Ramacharaka. She told me later that the very discovery of
those books which "revealed the existence of another world,
beyond the senses" was shrouded in mystery: one night, the
name of a bookshop that she did not know had appeared to her
in a dream. The next day her car had an accident in a secluded
street in Cape Town and when she looked up she saw that she
was in front of the bookshop of her dream. She went in and
studied the shelves on theosophy, occultism and yoga. She
bought only Ramacharaka's books. They had "opened India
to her".

For two days, I had to give up my long walks and I was unable
to dream or to think as had been my daily custom for so many

months. Jenny was still ill and needed me almost all the time. She realized that her company was not welcome to me but she felt so alone and so unhappy that she swallowed her self-respect and continually sent the warden to fetch me, on one pretext or another. She continued telling me about herself, for hours at a stretch, as though she felt it necessary to recount her whole life before she could communicate spiritually with me. She had first of all to clean out every corner of her soul before me. She believed she was different from her contemporaries: in fact, like so many of them, she lived in a perpetual romanticism, feeding on resplendent ideas of nobility and some grandiose notion of the 'Truth'.

Jenny told me of her contempt for the world, for society, the family and love. She spoke of the infinite suffering she had had to undergo before she had found her freedom by renouncing everything. Her renunciation of music, of art, had been the most painful. As for love, her experience had been too scanty to enable her to talk about it. She had never been in love. The man she thought she had loved had got engaged to another woman. She had understood that her love for him was nothing but an illusion. She had wanted to experience physical love before renouncing this ephemeral life and going off in search of the Absolute. So, two weeks before leaving Africa, she had given herself to a friend, a nice German boy, an excellent dancer who had wooed her a little. He had not believed her when she told him she was a virgin and his clumsy brutality had so disgusted her that she had determined never to know carnal love again. One thing enchanted her about the life she was planning: she would never have to love again or be loved. She truly believed every man to be a brute, a pig or an imbecile, and that the only males worthy of consideration were those who had renounced the 'pleasures' of the world – hermits, philosophers, mystics. Her mind was filled with a host of contradictory ideas, which had become tangled with her emotional disappointment and that common female superstition that makes a cult of the 'superior man', which glorifies adventure, renunciation, solitude.

As I listened to her, I was filled with something akin to fury. Since I had retired to the mountains I had trained myself to follow my thinking on any subject through to its conclusion, to examine an idea rigorously, to acknowledge all its implications. The incoherent arguments of this young woman in search of the Absolute and the mass of confused ideas which filled her mind were genuinely painful to me.

Whenever I went back to my room I noted down my judgements and impressions in my journal. It seemed to me that Jenny's arrival here was much more than a random incident; her presence signified my renewed contact with a universe and a way of thinking from whose grasp I had deliberately withdrawn.

After a week she was better and had regained her strength. She still did not leave. In the meantime, my attitude towards her had completely changed. At first, she had bored and irritated me. Now she interested me, much as a circus side-show might: she also enabled me to appreciate certain things at their true worth, particularly that European world which I had left and to which I would have, sooner or later, to return. Above all she allowed me to gauge my own life and values.

I have to admit that I was appalled when, surprising Jenny half-naked in her room one day, I realized that I felt no emotion. I looked at her as if she were a piece of furniture...

That night, I had much to reflect on... I wondered if my excessive love for Maitreyi, followed by the brutal shock of our separation and my present solitude, had not suffocated all masculine desire in me, transforming me into a kind of emotional eunuch. I asked myself if I had chosen to live away from the world simply because I was unable to confront it. I had decided to renounce love and women. But was that because neither love nor women had any more power to tempt me? I underwent hours of terrible anguish that night. I was frightened of becoming a human derelict, with the mechanical responses of an automaton, that I would bear the scars of my first disappointment for the rest of my life. It is true that women, the world – with its struggles, its illusions, its realities – no longer interested me. But I was inflamed with curiosity, I had to know whether the world and women could still interest me. Were my desire for isolation and my disgust for the world caused by my state of mind? Would I be, despite myself, forced to renounce everything and to run away? Or was I still free to choose?

I wanted to see Jenny with fresh eyes, but I did not experience the slightest excitement, the slightest stirring of anything resembling passion, in her presence. I had not reconquered my freedom.

I started setting traps for her, forcing her to become feminine, as she doubtless had been before she left Cape Town. Perhaps she would succeed in seducing me... If I obtained with her, from her, the proof that the man in me had not died, that I had stayed the same – with my faults, my weaknesses, my passions – then I could withdraw from the world, I would be free to do anything I wanted because I would know I had the power to do the opposite.

Jenny indeed began to be, on occasion, very feminine in my presence. She liked to hold forth on theosophy and the secrets of central Tibet and other such myths to which she gave naïve credence. She would half-shut her eyes and her voice would take on warmer tones. Or she would burst into fits of laughter, offering me, with great affection in her voice, a cup of chocolate – and, although she had renounced the use of all make-up since arriving in the mountains, she began putting a little powder on her face. She continually tried to make me tell her why I too had chosen this solitude and what my ring with the black stone signified.

Curiously, I often thought of Maitreyi when I looked at Jenny and spoke with her. It was the presence of Maitreyi and of her alone that I preserved in my mind. I often imagined myself kissing a woman, this Jenny for example, and my certainty that such a thing would be totally impossible amazed me. The idea of any amorous adventure seemed to me inconceivable, unreal. Indeed, I loved Maitreyi so fanatically, her memory eclipsed any other presence in my mind so completely, that my life, obsessively dedicated to the past, lost all dignity in my eyes, as though it had become irredeemably decayed. What would become of me? I had the impression that our love story was beginning to resemble that of Heloise and Abelard. I wanted to feel free again, to confirm once and for all my freedom, so that I could love Maitreyi again, without fearing that my love was forcing me into exile from life. It is very difficult for me to unravel, today, the tangled threads of the obscure emotions that led me to think that by having an affair I would be freeing myself of my chains. Indeed, I am not certain that I have fully understood it all.

Jenny had arranged her departure for the following Monday and had written to Ranikhet for a porter. In those last few days she began to make more and more insinuations, seizing the slightest pretext to smile knowingly at me, complaining that she was going to renounce a life that she hardly knew, declaring that she would have liked one single experience because nothing deserved to be repeated in love... I was highly amused by this sudden re-emergence of her femininity. On the Saturday evening the moonlight was magnificent. I decided to speak to her, in order to ascertain more clearly what was happening in me, to understand why there was so much I could not speak about, why I hid myself so assiduously. I would sit with her on the veranda and tell her, from beginning to end, the story of Maitreyi.

Around midnight we were overcome by cold and we went into her room to drink a cup of tea. I finished my story by summarising Khokha's letter and by affirming that I intended to forget Maitreyi, so that she would not suffer. I barely understood what I meant by this, but the phrase sounded well and I

said it. I, who usually take sincerity to absurd limits, play-acted
a little that night. Jenny said nothing, visibly sad, a tear on the
end of her eyelashes. I asked her why she was crying. She did
not reply. I went over to her, took her hands in mine, squeezed
her arm and asked her again. She did not speak. My face was
close to hers, our breath mingled and in a voice still quieter,
warmer, I repeated my question. She suddenly sighed deeply,
closed her eyes, took hold of my shoulders and kissed my lips
with a wild fervour.

It was with a curious sense of joy that I went to bolt the door
of the room.

These last pages seem to bear no relation to the story of Maitreyi and yet they are simply its continuation. As I held the
blonde, robust body of the Finnish Jewess in my arms, I
thought only of Maitreyi. It was Maitreyi I sought in every
one of my kisses; yet I also wanted to rid myself of her memory,
to annihilate it. As I covered the length of that milky white
body, which had known love only once and which love had
abandoned, I was in search of a single detail that would remind
me of Maitreyi. I knew very well that had I found it, I would
have been overcome with horror and disgust.

Did I want to forget Maitreyi or simply to prove to myself
that I loved her alone, that it would be impossible for me to love
anyone else? I no longer knew if it was an authentic experiment
or if it was the first distraction, the first descent into the mud... I
could not believe that such memories as mine were threatened
with annihilation. I could not accept that I was no different
from the wretched thousands who love and who forget and who
die without ever having considered anything as definitive,
eternal. A few weeks earlier I had felt so enslaved by my
passion, so certain of its omnipotence! But perhaps life itself,
like the story of my passion, is nothing but an enormous joke?

I interrogated myself in this way because I was frightened to
acknowledge the immensity, the power, of my love for

Maitreyi. Without doubt, Jenny's kisses had profoundly disgusted me. I was certain that it would be a long time before I mustered the courage to approach another woman! It would have to be in very different circumstances.

It was Maitreyi whom I loved, Maitreyi alone! I had had to grit my teeth as I invented all sorts of caresses that made the innocent Jenny swoon with delight – but which only excited my rage, because they did not numb my pain, or efface from the lively memory of my senses the other, the only one, Maitreyi.

"Why did you fall into my arms, earlier?" I asked the poor girl.

"I wanted you to love me also, as you loved Maitreyi," she replied, looking at me with her blue, expressionless eyes.

I said nothing. Was such a thirst for illusion possible? Such a desire for love? Yet I think she knew that I could never love her, not even with a carnal love.

"You told me how much you loved her and I thought of myself, alone and unhappy. I wanted to cry."

I left her room at dawn, atrociously rational. She lay sleeping on the bed; its indescribable disarray bore testament to my frenetic efforts to forget Maitreyi.

On the Monday, I escorted her as far as the torrent which crossed the pine forest. Why had the Lord put her in my path? Jenny Isaac, will I see you again, one day?

I was alone once again, disgusted with myself, stunned, not knowing what would happen to me, interested only in taking up my interrupted dream at Maitreyi's side. I have retained only a very vague memory of that time, of insomnia and empty days...

And then, suddenly, everything left. I awoke one morning, earlier than usual. Surprised, I looked, head up, at the sun, the light, the greenery. I was saved. I had been delivered from a sentence of death. I wanted to sing, to run. I do not know what caused the miracle. Something had descended upon me and had filled me. I was free to leave the mountain.

XV

Extracts from my diary:
I have been looking for work all day at the quayside offices. B—'s promise of a post as French translator at the consulate has not materialised. I have no more than a 100 rupees left – yet many people here owe me money. Harold is behaving atrociously. I asked him to let me sleep in his room – I have to move out on the fifteenth – and he refused, for an idiotic reason: I am no longer a Christian and he does not want to sleep in the same room as an idolater! The real reason is that he knows everything. He knows that I have no more money, nor any hope of a good salary. Mrs Ribeiro has forgotten all I've done for her and barely offers me a cup of tea when I am at Harold's. I have nothing left to sell. Depressing day. Too many problems, far too many...

I have seen Khokha again. He brought me another letter from Maitreyi. I refused to take it. I told him that I had given my word of honour to the engineer. (Did I in fact give it? I cannot even remember.) Khokha claims that Maitreyi insists on meeting me one day in the park at Bhowanipore or in a cinema. She wants to telephone me. I refused. I refuse everything, stubbornly. But inside I am suffering terribly. What is the good of starting it all again...? It can only end in tears and madness.

"Tell her to forget me. Her Alain? He is dead! She should not wait for him any longer!"

I wondered if there were some outrageousness I could commit that would deliver Maitreyi to me for ever but I could think of nothing. Run away with her... Yes, but how would I get her?

How could I enter the house at Bhowanipore once more, without crossing Sen's vigilant path?... And there is perhaps something else. Perhaps I have the feeling that I do not deserve her. Perhaps she will never understand my behaviour. I do not know. I do not know anything any more. I wish she would forget me, that she were not suffering. Our love is over.

Since yesterday morning she has been telephoning every hour: "Where is Alain? I want to speak to Alain! Tell him it is urgent, from Maitreyi, from his friend Maitreyi." My landlady is exasperated. She calls me. "Alain! Go and finish it once and for all with that brute of a negress!" I want to punch her in the mouth – but I smile. Savage fury inside. Suffering which grows, grows, until I cannot bear it any more. I fall to my knees. I scream, "Lord, enough!"

I was finishing a conversation with B— on the telephone today when I heard a voice on the line. With horror, I recognized it.... Maitreyi! "Alain! Why do you not want me to speak to you? Alain, have you forgotten?" I hung up. I had to cling to the furniture so as not to fall. Now I am languishing in my room. Lord, why can I not forget her? Why can this torture of hot coals not be over, once and for all? I want to do something that will disgust her, that will force her to forget me. I will live with a woman – with Gertie – and make sure Khokha tells Bhowanipore...

Negotiations with the Burma Oil Company. They need a river agent. I think I could do the job. I must get it. I worked at the Technical Institute library this afternoon, reading up on what the job would entail. The police have been after me twice already. They are constantly repatriating Europeans who are unemployed. If that happens, it will be the cruellest of defeats...

Looking through my papers today, I came across the letter which a stranger had sent to Maitreyi, on her birthday, accom-

panied by a magnificent bouquet. An insane desire to read it
took hold of me. As I still haven't totally mastered Bengali, I
asked a pharmacist to translate it for me. It says: "O my
unforgettable light of day, I cannot come to see you today. I
can only see you alone, for me alone, like the day when I held
you in my arms and that day..."
 I cannot copy any more. I feel impossible, inhuman jealousy.
I could bang my head against the wall. Let her telephone me,
right now! Oh yes! I would like that! My God! How could I
have been taken in? Must the world always catch me out?

I did not write much more in my diary. I hope to have done with
India soon. I have some offers of work, without contract, but
certain, at Singapore. I don't yet know what I will have to do
there but they are advancing the cost of the journey. I have not
told anyone. I have already bragged too much about finding
work so easily...

I have broken off completely with Harold. If Clara had not been
there, I would have slaughtered him. I have a terrible desire to
fight. Gertie has quarrelled with Clara over the incident. Since
I have moved into Gertie's room we are taken for the happiest
couple in the world. People think we have secretly married. But
Gertie knows the truth. I can love only Maitreyi and if I am
living with her, it is for revenge.

Khokha has come asking for me several times. I left a note
saying he should be thrown out. He sends me letters, written
in atrocious English, which I only half read. He tells me constantly that Maitreyi is determined to commit some act of
madness so that she is thrown out and can join me. I shudder
at the thought. I deliberately avoid thinking about it and reso-
lutely push out of my mind anything that might remind me of
Bhowanipore. Khokha declares that she is capable of giving

herself to anyone so that she will be thrown on to the street and can be with me again. Romantic nonsense?

Singapore. I meet J—, the nephew of Mrs Sen. He works for a large printing company. Joy, greetings, memories. He is the first acquaintance I've run into here. I invite him to dinner. After several cigarettes, he looks me straight in the eyes and says, in a serious tone:

"Alain, you know Maitreyi loved you very much? Everyone knew about it..."

I tried to stop him. If it is pleasant to meet someone from over there, I cannot bear condolences or comments on my affair... I know people found out many things and it is a great shame!

But he insists.

"No, let me go on, I have some bad news to tell you."

"She is not dead?"

I was horror-struck – but without real conviction because I am certain that, if Maitreyi is to die before me, I will instinctively know the exact moment of her death.

"It would be better if she were dead! She has committed a shameful act. She gave herself to the fruit seller..."

I want to shout, scream, roar with laughter. I grip the table. I am on the point of fainting. J— sees my distress and puts his hand on my arm to comfort me.

"It was a very hard blow for us all. Little Mama has almost gone mad with suffering. Maitreyi has gone to Midnapore, to give birth... Supposedly in secret. But everyone knows. They have tried to buy off the wretch. The case has gone to court..."

I understand nothing. Even now I have not grasped it. The case?

I ask if they have thrown Maitreyi out.

"Sen will not hear of her being thrown out. He says that he would rather kill her himself than let her run off. They want her to study. I am not very sure. Philosophy perhaps. They were keeping her for a good match. But now almost the whole story

is out... who would take her? Yet they don't want to throw her
out. Maitreyi shouts at them continually, 'Why do you not give
me to the dogs? Why do you not throw me on the street?' I
think she has gone mad. How else could she have done such a
thing?"

For hours on end, I have been thinking. I can decide on
nothing. Telegraph Narendra Sen? Write to Maitreyi?

I sense she committed that act of madness for me. If I had
read the letters that Khokha brought me! Perhaps she had a
plan... My soul is troubled, very troubled... And yet I want to
write everything, everything.

And what if it had all been nothing but some huge farce? A
fine trick played on me by my passion? Do I have to I accept it
all, believe it all, without reservation? What do I know of the
truth?

I would like to be able to look Maitreyi in the eyes...

January, February 1933